Karleigh
A Story of Faith

Lisa Washington

Library of Congress Control Number:

ISBN-13: 978-0-9998871-7-2
ISBN-10: 0-9998871-7-2

Washington Way Publishing
P.O. Box 7231
Fishers, IN 46038
Printed in the United States of America
www.thewashingtonwayllc.com

For My Niece

Carleigh Christine

Be joyful in hope, patient in affliction, faithful in prayer.
Romans 12:12 NIV

ALSO BY LISA WASHINGTON

THE FAITH SERIES

When You Least Expect It

More Than You Know

Love Lifted Me

ACKNOWLEDGMENTS

My Lord and Savior, Jesus Christ

My Husband, Mr. Washington

Rasheda Randle, Ivy League Consulting

My Beta Readers ~ G. Topp, L. Davenport, S. Futrell

Chapter 1

What happens to a dream deferred?

Karleigh arrived at an empty parking lot and a soon to be parking space designated just for her. The building in front of her was not as old as the surrounding neighborhood, but not as new as the recent construction happening nearby.

The building in front of her would become her new hair salon. After months of planning and saving, Serenity Hair Salon and Spa was finally becoming a reality.

She parked her car directly facing the doors of the single-level building where she could see the reflection of her headlights in the windows. Her old Toyota had seen good and bad days, today was a good day. It had been with her since her years in college. The little red bucket, as her sisters affectionately named it, still carried her to and from with no problems.

Sitting in the quiet of the parking lot stirred many different emotions within Karleigh. Doubt, stress, anxiety, but the most prevailing emotion, was fear. Could she do this? Could she be successful following her dreams? Starting a business was scary for most people, but when she listened to her pastor preach about stepping out on faith and paying attention to the signs that God was putting all around, directing your path, she knew what she had to do.

Over the years, she had dreamed of owning her own salon. She wanted more than anything to be her own boss. Her younger sisters had started their own businesses a few years ago. Karmyn owned a fitness gym, and Kaleigh had a real estate firm. Karleigh hated to admit she was a little jealous of her sister's success. But now, it was finally time for her to add *entrepreneur* to a shortlist of her accomplishments.

Karleigh watched other people step out on faith and try something new with their lives and careers. She was too afraid to do the same thing. The confidence she had within herself wavered at times. She never felt smart enough to try to take on a business like a salon. Karleigh often thought other people did it bigger and better. The "it" could be almost anything and unfortunately impacted her decisions. Ultimately, she was afraid to fail.

Her sisters often told her, as the oldest, she was the strongest. She had the strongest faith of them all. But, many times, Karleigh didn't feel she was strong at all. In her mind, being strong meant going after what you wanted in life; and for years, she didn't.

Struggling with insecurities and self-esteem issues caused Karleigh to have to present a strong front. Her sisters didn't even know her most inward thoughts about herself. She felt awkward around other business people and unsure of herself. She was good at encouraging and motivating others to live out their ideas, while her own dreams laid dormant in her mind.

Not anymore. Karleigh was ready to leave behind the unappreciative bosses of the world and the nosey co-workers. This was her time to step out on faith and shine brightly. So why did she feel completely overwhelmed and scared to death that her dream of entrepreneurship would not work out in her favor?

Karleigh had saved every extra penny she earned over the years to be able to afford her own salon. Years of penny-pinching, couponing, and going without the fun things in life, just to see her dream come true.

However, every time Karleigh thought she had the money to place a deposit on a location, something would happen. The first time, her car needed repairs that she could barely afford, causing her to have to take the bus to work for a month. The next time, she thought she was ready, she had an emergency appendectomy, and her health insurance had a $5,000 deductible that she had to pay upfront.

Everything she struggled with to get to this point was all worth it in the end. Karleigh managed to stay the course on her journey to entrepreneurship.

Now, she sat in her car, afraid to walk through the doors she worked so hard to open. No one understood her desire to work for herself, to be independent, except for her sisters. Her parents supported each of their girls from afar. Meaning, they would do the minimum required to be considered supportive parents.

She wasn't ungrateful; she loved her parents. Their beliefs and attitudes were from an old school way of thinking. They believed you went to college, got a job, and worked for the same company for 20-30 years, then retired. Karleigh and her sisters had different beliefs. They believed in following your passion and purpose. She remembered hearing someone say, if you love what you do, you will never work a day in your life.

Karleigh watched her parents work for other people all of their lives. Never had they wanted to work for themselves. Her mother was a skilled seamstress but worked for 20 years as a social worker for the state. Karleigh had once seen her mother create a beautiful wedding gown and the joy that brought to her. Sewing was her passion, but she chose the stability of a full-time job.

Her father was an accountant. While he loved his job, he often wished he had the flexibility of owning his own CPA firm. He had missed significant milestones in his daughter's lives due to work commitments. Instead of leaving the company he worked for and starting his own, he chose to stay and deal with incompetent managers and leadership. He decided to retire when his manager, 20 years his junior, tried to chastise his work performance in front of other staff members. With his daughters all grown and out of the house, he knew it was time to throw in the towel.

For some people, the love from her parents and paid college education was support enough, but what Karleigh needed was for her parents to say she was doing the right thing. She needed reassurance that she had their support. Sure, her father gave her an interest-free loan to start her business, but never had he said, "I believe in you." She wanted and needed that comforting from her parents.

Even without their reassurance, she was comforted in her faith. Holding the metal key in her hands was proof that prayer does work. Karleigh had prayed about this day for so long. The building owners had given her the keys earlier in the day, and still, she couldn't believe everything that was finally happening.

She had started to give up on her dream after her appendectomy, but her sisters wouldn't let her. She remembered Poe telling her to "stop putting a period where God had put a comma." Her sister's favorite saying was, "And, this too, shall pass." And it had. Karleigh and Poe had prayed together for months.

Poe's real name was Kaleigh Patience Hammond. She was the positive and praying sister. As a kid, she hated having a K name and decided to call herself Poe after her favorite writer, Edgar Allen Poe. Since then, the name just stuck with her.

Poe was also the sister who they often joked about being the closest to God. When her sisters wanted to hang out with friends or party, Poe was studying bible stories. History fascinated Poe, and the bible was full of history. She was also the singer of the family and probably knew every gospel song there was.

When Karleigh didn't know how she would afford her own salon, Poe was the sister that told her, "where there is a will, there is a way." Karleigh held on to that saying and believed in it more than she believed in herself.

She had taken her savings, cashed in a few old bonds, and obtained a loan from her father to be able to make her salon happen. She prayed she had enough money left over for the renovations. The renovations she needed were mostly cosmetic; new paint, a new floor, a few rugs, and decorative items would have the place looking like an upscale salon.

Karleigh took a deep breath and finally reached for the car door. Before she could step out of her car and walk into her future, her cell phone rang. The musical ringtone of Missy Elliott's *"Work it"* indicated that the caller was her sister, Karmyn.

"Hello, sister," Karleigh answered the call with a little annoyance in her voice. She had wanted to be alone for this moment. Starting her own

business was a huge step, and she wasn't ready to share the moment with anyone just yet. Growing up, the oldest of four sisters, she had to share everything from her clothes to her toys to her time. Just this once, she wanted to be alone with something that belonged solely to her.

"Did you get the keys?" Karmyn asked, full of excitement.

"Yep, I'm sitting in front of the building right now."

"I'm so excited for you sister," Karmyn excitedly expressed. Her tone, then, changed to a warm feel, "But, I hope you are not planning to go into that building alone."

Karmyn Hope Hammond was the third oldest of the sisters and, she was the mother hen, often forgetting she was younger. But, what Karmyn could do, without effort, was see to the needs in others. She had a way of caring about people by interfering in their lives.

"Your silence means you are alone. Do not go into that building by yourself. I'm on my way. Promise me you won't enter without us?"

"Us?" Karleigh was afraid that meant her sisters, and maybe even her parents were on their way over.

"Yes, Poe is with me, and Kyna is on her way there from work. We knew you would try to be alone, but it ain't happening, baby. Bye." Karmyn disconnected the call.

Kyna Love Hammond was the baby of the family and loved every minute of it. Karmyn treated her like a baby doll when she was born. She was the sister that could do no wrong. She was also the most loving sister, just like her name.

Karleigh rolled her eyes when she disconnected the call. She loved her sisters, but sometimes, it was nice to have peace. Seeing as it was pretty late on a Sunday evening, and she was the only other car in the parking lot, she decided to heed her sister's advice this time and wait for them to arrive. Within five minutes, Kyna was pulling her red Camaro into the parking spot next to Karleigh. Karmyn and Poe were pulling up right behind her.

The Hammond sisters looked like quadruplets, despite having ten years between the oldest and youngest. Karleigh hugged each of her sisters, and then, the foursome started screaming with excitement. Karleigh had shared her dream with her sisters while growing up, and now, she had the keys in her hand.

The sisters held hands as they walked toward the front door. Karleigh stared at their reflection in the window for a few seconds before she used her key to enter the building. This was it, her moment. She opened the door, and their excitement dwindled down a little when they were immediately hit with a stale odor, and Poe started sneezing.

"How long has this space been empty? Geesh, it stinks in here," Kyna complained.

"And, it's super dusty," Poe sneezed again.

Karleigh moved to the back of the first open space and flipped a switch. The owners had told her the electricity and water would be on for 30 days to allow her to begin renovations and get the utilities switched into her name. The lights flickered on in a ripple effect until every light illuminated the space. Her heart filled with love. The room was empty and dusty, but it belonged to her, and she would make it beautiful. Serenity Hair Salon would live.

Karmyn moved closer to Karleigh and put an arm around her waist. Karleigh was grateful for the support. She would never tell them, but she was glad her sisters were there with her. Kyna and Poe took their cue and walked over to embrace their sisters in one big group hug. They understood Karleigh's dream better than anyone.

Their parents were great, but they had their own dreams for each of the girls' lives. Kevin and Kyra Hammond gently tried to steer each of them into professions they thought best suited their daughters' personalities. But, each sister had a different passion, except for Kyna. Kyna did just as she was told and became a nurse.

Karleigh moved from her sister's embrace and walked toward the back of the ample, open space to check out the restrooms and the private area where she would place her private booth and office. She needed a secluded area away from the main space for her older clients. Those that didn't want other people to know they wore weaves or wigs. The younger generation didn't care that other people knew the long, flowing tresses were braided, sewed, or glued onto their heads.

The sisters continued to assess the area, making mental notes of the work that needed to be done. They would need paint, new carpet, wall décor, mirrors, cabinets, and a ton of other decorative items to make it look like an upscale salon. Karleigh had been collecting some of those items over the years and placing them in a storage unit. She had enough salon chairs, mirrors, and cabinets to have at least five additional stylists.

At the moment, she only had a contract with one stylist who doubled as an esthetician. Jasmine and Karleigh attended cosmetology school together. Jasmine had moved to Tampa for a few years and was now coming back home to marry the love her life. The timing worked out perfectly for them both.

"Tomorrow, the transformation will begin," Karleigh said to herself.

*****

Simon Sharpe of the Sharper Image Barbershops was excited about the possibility of expanding his first location. Sharper Image had several locations across the city, but Simon wanted to expand his first barbershop into spa services for men. The neighborhood was changing, and Simon thought a spa for men would fit right in. He wanted to add services like an esthetician, a nail technician, and a massage therapist. Men may not come out and say it, but they enjoyed being pampered just like women.

His first barbershop location was his home-base. It is where he spent most of his time. There was a connection to the neighborhood that he couldn't let go of there. It was his baby, and he nurtured and watched it grow to the success it was today.

His barbershops were usually closed on Sundays and Mondays, but Simon made exceptions for his high-profile clients. Nicolas Butler wasn't only a celebrity attorney, specializing in crisis management, but also Simon's fraternity brother. Simon laughed to himself, thinking about the shenanigans he and Nick would get into during their years in college.

When he arrived at his flagship location, he noticed there were cars in the parking lot. That was odd for a Sunday evening. There were three domestic cars, and he knew neither of them belonged to Nick. Nicolas drove a foreign model sports car.

Simon pulled into his reserved parking space and noticed the lights on in the building next to his. The building space was supposed to be empty. It was a part of his expansion plans. The last time he talked to the building owners, they were on board with his ideas, or at least he thought.

Simon got out of his car and approached the building. He noticed four women walking around and inspecting the space. He didn't want to startle the ladies, but he needed to know what was going on. He tried to make some noise as he approached. One of the women turned and made direct eye contact with him. Simon pointed to the door, asking for permission to enter, holding his hands up to show that he wasn't a threat.

The other ladies turned around and looked from one to the other. The taller of the four women nodded for him to enter. Simon noticed that the women all resembled one another. Clearly, they were related and must have been sisters he deduced.

"Hello, ladies. I'm sorry to interrupt. My name is Simon Sharpe, I'm the owner of the Sharper Image Barbershop next door," he introduced himself.

The ladies just stared at him. If he wasn't mistaken, one lady had the outward appearance of shock, and one showed complete distrust on her face. He was feeling uncomfortable under their scrutinous eyes.

"I'm sorry. Hi, Simon. It's nice to meet you. My name is Karleigh Hammond." She stepped forward and extended her hand. "These are my sisters. I'm the new owner of Serenity Hair Salon and Spa," Karleigh released his hand and motioned around the space.

Simon felt a subtle shudder run through his arm when he shook her hand. He also noticed she had long, beautiful fingers and soft caressing hands. He disengaged his hand at that thought. He had no idea why he was paying attention to her hands and fingers.

He shoved his hands into his pockets so he couldn't reach out to touch her again. "Serenity Hair Salon and Spa? Right here?" he asked, confused and angry. He had plans for this space. It sat empty for over a year, and he was ready for his expansion. The floorplan blueprints had just arrived, and he had an appointment set up with the building owners for Monday morning.

"Yes, I just received the keys today," Karleigh answered with excitement.

"Interesting. Very interesting," Simon said, under his breath. "Congratulations, Karleigh. It was a pleasure to meet you all. Good night."

Simon left the building quickly and walked next door to his shop just as Nick was pulling into the parking lot. He waited as Nick took his time stepping out of his insanely expensive sports car, adjusted his clothes, and surveyed the area to see if there was anyone around who noticed him. Nick's ego was larger than most skyscrapers, but he was a cool guy once you got to know him.

The high-profile attorney also specialized in divorces for the elite, among other things. The local, professional sports industry kept him in business. Occasionally, he would take a case pro-bono to make himself feel good about the exorbitant amount of money he charged his clients. Nick wasn't a total jerk, he also did a lot of volunteer work he didn't like to brag about.

"How are you doing, Simon?" Nick asked, removing his suit jacket as he entered the shop.

"Living my best days, brother. Glad you're here; I have some business I need to discuss with you."

Nick walked over and sat in Simon's chair, located in the rear of the open space of the barbershop. Simon wrapped a cape around Nick's neck in preparation for his customary haircut and shave. He was glad that his fraternity brother and his personal attorney was the client of the evening because he needed advice.

"Nick, you know I've been talking with the building owners about expanding this location into the building next door, right?" Simon started the conversation.

"Yeah. I remember you mentioning it. So, how's that going?" Nick asked while checking messages on his phone.

"Well, I just found out the building owners leased the building to a new salon." Saying it out loud had Simon getting angry all over again.

Nick being the lawyer that he was asked the obvious question, "Did you have a contract in place?"

"No. I was just discussing the possibilities with the owners. Nothing formal was put into place, yet. You would have been the first to know, as my attorney."

"Yeah, well, I thought maybe you got another attorney to handle business for you. I hate to tell you this, but you have no recourse. Until the salon's lease is up, and hope they don't renew, don't plan to expand this location."

Nick confirmed what Simon was thinking. There was nothing he could do, and all his planning and preparation were down the drain. It was his own fault for not jumping on the deal right away. He should have, at least, given the owners a deposit.

Simon continued with Nick's haircut and shave while they talked about his latest client. The sound of the clippers buzzing was kind of euphoric for him. Simon could probably do a perfect cut with his eyes closed. He had been cutting Nick's hair in the same bald fade since their days in undergrad.

What if something happened to her salon before she opened? That thought came from nowhere, and Simon immediately squashed it. There was no way he was going to sabotage her salon. His Christian values didn't have him doing things in that manner. If anything at all, he would wait her out. He had waited this long, another year to see if she became successful wouldn't hurt. And, if she were successful, then he would make other plans.

"Have you thought about expanding one of your other locations?" Nick asked.

Simon had never thought about his other barbershops. They were smaller and not located in his target market for the male spa. His other locations offered services geared toward school-aged young men. They were decorated with signage of pop culture and played current music. For the spa, his vision for expansion would cater to older men who valued self-care.

"I don't think my idea would do well in those locations," Simon responded.

"You're probably right about that. Have you met the salon owner yet?" still scrolling through emails on his phone.

"Yeah, she and her sisters are over there now checking out the place. She seems really excited."

"Did you say…sisters? Well, let's get this haircut moving along. Maybe they will still be there when we're finished."

Simon laughed. Nick's ego had him believing no woman could resist his charm, his smile, or his designer suits. Simon preferred less flashy methods to attract women. Recently, he hadn't wanted to draw any women to him.

His clients, barbershops, and community service kept him pretty busy. His parents made sure that serving the community and giving back was a must in his legacy.

Legacy was important in the Sharpe family. It meant more than the amount of money or land you left for future generations. It also meant that the contributions and the name you would leave for years to come had meaning. The Sharpe legacy was steeped in philanthropy. Simon's great, great-grandfather, Luther Sharpe, had founded the city's first children's hospital in 1870. His grandfather was a member of the Disabled American Veterans and the American Legion. Grandpa Harold Sharpe gave everything he had of himself, after family, to fight for veterans' rights.

His father, Romell Sharpe, had a passion for the community. There was never a homeless person or a single mother in need that Romell didn't find some way to assist. He still worked at the church food pantry and the homeless coalition every day, even though he retired years ago. Simon's mother served right alongside her husband. They were happy that way.

*****

After Simon abruptly left, Karleigh looked incredulously at her sisters.

"Well, that was strange, don't you think?" Karleigh asked her sisters.

"Do you know who that was?" Kyna asked in response.

"I guess we should know, so, please tell us," Karmyn said.

Kyna rolled her eyes at her sister's sarcastic remark and continued talking. "That was Simon Sharpe. Thee Simon Sharpe."

When the sisters didn't get as excited as Kyna, she tried again. "Simon Sharpe…only the wealthiest bachelor in this city. You guys really don't know who he is?"

"Sorry, sister; his name doesn't ring a bell," Karleigh said.

"He's wealthy from owning a barbershop? I need to switch businesses," Poe added.

"See, that's why I don't hang around you old women anymore. Simon Sharpe owns several upscale barbershops, and his family comes from money. Plus, he has made some good investments." Kyna offered.

"Dang, Kyna, do you know his whole biography?" Poe joked with her. Kyna didn't seem to find it amusing.

"Never mind. It's pointless telling you three anything. I'm leaving. Love you, sisters."

Once Kyna left the building, the three sisters waited for a beat, then burst into laughter. Because of the age difference, they often teased their baby sister. Kyna often called her sisters "old ladies" when they didn't get as excited about a subject as she did. Storming away was definitely Kyna's style.

Chapter 2

Simon was still a little angry about the building situation. Early Monday morning, he sat in the lobby of the offices of Dorsey Real Estate, the owner of his building. He wanted answers, even though he was fully aware that there was nothing that would change. Point blank, she had a contract, and he didn't.

Jeff and Brad entered together about 30 minutes after Simon arrived. The brothers had been in real estate for over 40 years. They reminded Simon of the Mortimer and Randolph Duke, characters from the movie *Trading Places*. Simon smiled whenever he had to meet with the brothers.

"Simon, were we expecting you this morning? Come on into my office," Jeff said. Jeff handed his jacket to his secretary while Brad did the same. They had offices that faced each other at the end of a narrow hallway. Each had their own secretary and personal assistant.

Brad followed Simon into his brother's office and took a seat on the leather sofa that sat against the wall with the door. Simon was frustrated because the brothers seemed to forget they had an appointment that morning. He was sure they knew he wanted to talk about leasing that building.

"So, what brings you by on a Monday morning?" Brad asked. Jeff sat behind his large wooden desk and motioned for Simon to have a seat.

"Well, Mr. Dorsey, it's about the building next door to my location on Jefferson street. That building sat empty for over a year, and I was hoping to lease it from you and expand my location."

Jeff looked at Brad. The two brothers seemed to be silently communicating with one another. Something like that twin telepathy Simon had heard about.

Simon was beginning to feel uncomfortable under their steady gaze and their ensuing silence. He shifted in his chair to attempt to look more relaxed. The attempt failed when he felt a small bead of sweat materialize on his brow.

"For Heaven's sake Brad, tell the young man," Jeff laughed.

"Simon, we knew you were interested in the building," Brad started.

"Then, why didn't someone tell me you were planning to lease it to another business?"

Jeff stood from his position on the sofa and walked to Simon, placing his frail hand on Simon's shoulder, he said, "We decided that another type of business was needed in that particular neighborhood."

"There are no hair salons within 15 miles. And, my Marcy, God bless her soul, would always complain about having to go so far for a good wash and cut." Brad stood and continued, "There will be other locations for you, Simon. We figured you would understand us deciding that Ms. Hammond deserved an opportunity to begin her business alongside you."

Simon watched the two men eye each other again. The brothers had given Simon his first opportunity when they leased the building to him. He had no collateral and no credit to offer, just a passion for making something good happen in that community.

Unlike the Duke brothers from the movie, the Dorsey brothers were kind-hearted and respectable men with high moral values. Simon respected their decision. He stood to shake each of their hands before leaving and heading to his office to sulk. Had he not waited so long to make his move on the building, he wouldn't feel the way he did. But like the saying, the early bird catches the worm, Simon had just slept a little too long.

Not many vehicles were in the parking lot when Simon arrived at his barbershop. He immediately noticed Karleigh's car parked right in front of her new salon and a few white panel vans. *She didn't waste any time getting started on her renovations*, he thought. Simon took his time getting out of his car and walking toward the front door of his shop, accepting his fate that an expansion of his place would not be happening any time soon.

A mass of curls came from nowhere and stepped right in his face. Simon had to do a double-take to realize that it was Karleigh yelling something at him. He first noticed how her hair was thick and long. Bouncy curls fell below her shoulder and around her face. A face that was apparently very angry with him.

"I know it was you. Why would you do that?" she sneered.

"What did I do?" Simon asked.

She poked her finger in his chest. "You called Mr. Dorsey? You don't want me to open my salon here?"

"I never said any such thing."

"So, you don't deny calling Mr. Dorsey? Unbelievable!" She turned to walk away.

"Karleigh," he yelled after her. "I didn't call them. I just went to their office to inquire about another building. I had plans for your building, but you beat me to it."

She turned around, causing her hair to flow in the breeze like she was in a Beyoncé video. The anger eased from her eyes, but he could see the uncertainty remained. The way the sunlight beamed from behind gave her a glow that made her appear angelic. She was absolutely stunning. No make-up, no jewelry…a natural beauty.

"So, you mean to tell me you didn't tell Mr. Dorsey that you wanted me out?"

"Absolutely not. I can't say that I am ecstatic about you being here, but I was slow to grab this location, and that's my fault. I can't be mad at you about that, now can I?"

Her shoulders dropped, and she appeared defeated. Why did her reaction cause Simon to feel the need to comfort her? He reached his hand toward her face and quickly snatched it back.

"Simon, I'm not normally a basket-case like this. I apologize for making accusations. It's just… when Ms. Norma said you were complaining about the building, I just…Never mind. Have a great day." Karleigh stalked off.

Interesting. Very interesting, Simon thought.

*****

"Why do I have to make a fool of myself? Especially in front of Simon," Karleigh admonished herself. She immediately made assumptions when Ms. Norma, the secretary for Jeff Dorsey, called her. Karleigh was known for having selective hearing; she often only heard part of a conversation before jumping to conclusions.

She thought Ms. Norma called to tell her how Simon was complaining about her business. But, now that she tried to remember the conversation, Ms. Norma had said something about Simon being upset about his business.

She quickly returned to her building only to find the workers had stopped working. They looked apprehensive and downright afraid. What would they have to be scared of? Had they heard the way she nearly attacked Simon.

"What's wrong? She asked.

The lead contractor spoke up, "It seems you have a bigger problem. We opened the wall on the left like you instructed and found the electrical wiring is not up to code. We are going to have to strip the entire building and replace all of the wirings."

"Oh no! how much is that going to cost?"

"Rough estimate, close to $3,200."

Karleigh felt her stomach turn over in knots. Instantly, her head was pounding. She had no idea where she was going to come up with another $3,200. She massaged her temples with the palm of her hands and tried not to cry.

The contractor was still talking. All Karleigh could hear was $3,200. Of all things to happen, electrical issues were something she could not ignore.

"Karleigh!"

"What? What more is there?" she snapped at him.

18

"I was saying that you probably won't have to pay for those repairs. Check with your building contract. The owners should have to take care of it for you."

Twice, in less than 30 minutes, Karleigh had embarrassed herself and felt like a fool. Just once, she wanted to listen first and react second. Her stress was self-imposed.

Karleigh went into her office to find her contracts. She prayed that the contractor was correct, and she wouldn't have to take on that expense. Shuffling through her papers, her mind started wandering back to her encounter with Simon. He was so handsome early in the morning. His smile, alone, caused Karleigh's pulse to race. She had to tell herself over and over again that she was not his type.

Men like Simon were usually seen with model types of women; tall, shapely, and beautiful. Karleigh wasn't unattractive by any means, but she seemed to only attract guys with low self-esteem, or the ones who thought too much of themselves. She just couldn't seem to find the middle ground.

She dismissed her thoughts of Simon and continued to look for her contracts. Soon enough, she retrieved her documents, and her thoughts drifted back to Simon. His lovely smile and piercing dark eyes haunted her.

From what she could find out on the internet, Simon Sharpe was a businessman in the tech industry before turning his talents into barbering. He had been a rising star in his field, then suddenly, he left it all behind. During her research, she could find no reason why a tech genius would do that.

Karleigh thought, maybe he was following his passion just as she was. She, too, had left a lucrative job in corporate America in search of something more significant and more fulfilling to her life.

She also found pictures of Simon at various charity events. He was mentioned as being a mentor to young men, an advocate for literacy programs, and a primary sponsor of the Dove House for Abused Women. She smiled at the thought that Simon must be one of the last good guys on the planet.

Chapter 3

Week one of renovations had come to an end. Karleigh had seen Simon only once in passing. She wanted to apologize for her earlier assumptions but was also trying to remain focused on her to-do list. The building owners were taking care of the issues within the walls of the building, she was continuing to stress over the other areas.

She was running low on funds in her bank account for the renovations. She had grossly underestimated the amount of work and the cost of that work. Karleigh was toying with the idea of asking her sisters to provide some sweat labor to help her finish. Karmyn would sign up for whatever was needed. Poe would probably help out if it didn't interfere with her own work. Kyna was the sister that would probably say no.

Karleigh thought about asking Simon but quickly dismissed the idea. They had just met last week. She didn't want him thinking she wasn't prepared to be in business for herself. She shouldn't care what he thought about her or her business sense. But, for some reason, she did care.

It was a Saturday night, and Karleigh was sitting in an empty room, with only her laptop, going over the floor tiles for the central area of the salon. The floor tiles were being ordered from a wholesaler in Richmond. They had the best prices and a vast selection to choose from. Karmyn recommended this company after using them for the floor tiles in her house.

After looking at pages and pages of floor tiles, the pages started to blend together. It was going to be near impossible for Karleigh to decide before the end of the night. She shut down her computer and decided she would make a final decision the next day. She was tired and had accomplished a lot for the day.

Sundays, in her family, were tradition. The entire Hammond family attended church and, then went directly to her parents' house for dinner. After dinner, the family would engage in some sort of movie, game, or lively debate that usually took the entire evening. Sunday dinners were a requirement, and only Kyna was ever exempt. Being a nurse, she would be on call and had to go to the hospital at a moment's notice.

Karleigh decided to enlist the assistance of her mother to help select the tiles. Whatever her mother chose would be the tile she would go with. That solved that problem, and she checked it off her to-do list. She leaned back in her folding chair and closed her eyes. She wanted to relax a little before going home.

Suddenly, her chair gave way from beneath her, and she went crashing to the floor with a loud scream. Jeremy, one of the last workers to leave, heard the commotion and rushed into her office. Karleigh tried to get up, accepting Jeremy's hand and placing her right hand on the ground for balance. She was surprised to find her hand submerged in water.

"What in the world is this?"

"Looks like it is coming from the wall," Jeremy went to inspect the area.

"No, No, No! This can't be happening."

"I'm going to have to open the wall to see where the leak is coming from."

Jeremy left the office and came back with a sledgehammer. With two hits, Jeremy found a busted pipe in the wall. Karleigh wanted to cry. This was yet another setback to her plan. Instead of breaking down in front of Jeremy, she found her phone and searched for a 24-hour plumber.

While they waited for the plumber to arrive, Jeremy put a temporary fix on the problem. The water was still leaking, just not gushing like before.

Karleigh was grateful that Jeremy was still in the building. She wasn't sure what she would have done had he not been there.

The plumber arrived about 3 hours later and put another temporary fix on the pipe. He informed her that the water pressure in the building would be low until she was able to get the pipes replaced. Another issue that was not budgeted for. She just hoped this would also be covered by the building owners.

*****

Simon was finishing with one of his pro-athlete clients. This guy liked to have a fresh haircut right before going to any party and before every game. It was close to midnight when his client left. Simon went to the restroom to wash his hands and found the water trickling out. He checked his other sinks and found the same thing. Simon was about to call a plumber when he saw Karleigh had a plumber at her location.

His first thought was, *why is she still there so late?* Then he thought, maybe something happened. He locked up his shop and walked over to her building just as the plumber was leaving. She was locking up, also.

"Hey, everything okay over here?" he asked.

"Of course. Why would you ask?" Karleigh responded.

"Because it's midnight, and you are just leaving. Plus, I have no water pressure in my shop, and the plumber is leaving. You sure everything is okay?"

"Fine, it's not okay. There is a burst pipe inside my wall. I'm sorry, I didn't know it affected your water also. The plumber promised he would be here first thing Monday morning to replace the pipes. I hope this doesn't interfere with your business."

Simon noticed the unshed tears in her eyes and her steady resolve, trying to hold it together. "Well, the good thing is, we are not open on Sundays, and any clients I may have can go to another location. We will be okay."

They stood there, staring at each for a few seconds. Neither saying a word. Simon was wondering what she was thinking. He was about to ask her a question about the pipes when she started talking first.

"Well, Simon, I'll see you around, I guess." She walked away to get in her car and drive away.

Simon wasn't sure what it was about Karleigh that caused him to get tongue-tied at that moment. He usually had witty come-backs or great one-liners. But around her, he could hardly remember his name.

He started to think that maybe she had heard about the media version of Simon Sharpe. The wealthy tech guy turned barber or the philanthropist who never dated the same woman twice. Neither of these descriptions was accurate.

Simon was just a regular guy who wanted to do what was right. And opening the barbershop was the right thing to do for him.

Chapter 4

Simon arrived at his barbershop early on a Thursday morning. It had been three weeks since he met Karleigh and her sisters. Since then, her salon had been a flurry of activity. She had construction crews over there nonstop. He heard from one of his barbers that her workers had found other issues within the walls of her building.

He hoped it wasn't too bad. Being a new business owner was tough, but to add unexpected repairs on top of everything, could be discouraging. He wanted to check in on her progress, but whenever they passed each other in the parking lot, she always seemed rushed.

He remembered when he moved into his first and current location, he didn't have the money for a renovation. He had bought some items from second-hand stores and even "lifted" a few things from some alleys here and there. He could only afford a gallon of paint once a month, so his walls took about ten months to completely paint.

Marquez had been working for Simon since the Sharper Image first opened. A few months later, Tyrel joined the shop. Since those first days, other barbers would come and go, but Tyrel and Marquez stayed the course.

Marquez was older than Simon by five years but acted more like an old man in his sixties. He claimed he had been around and seen a lot. At only 42 years of age, Marquez had five children by three different women named Paula. They joked that he only dated women with that name. Truthfully, it was just a strange coincidence.

Tyrel was 31 years old and had no children. What Simon liked most about him, was that he, also, had no drama. If he did have any issues with women, he kept it far from the barbershop. Every year in August, Tyrel would take a three-week vacation and return in a somber mood. It was something he never talked about.

Roxanne was the new barber. She was fresh from barber school but had been cutting hair in the neighborhood since her teenage years. She also specialized in dreadlocks, which brought a lot of the neighborhood kids around.

Simon didn't mind the neighborhood kids hanging around the shop if it kept them out of trouble. He had three flat-screen televisions installed and connected each of them to a gaming station to keep the kids entertained in the lobby while they waited. A few times a year, Simon would host a men's night, all-nighter. Boys ages 8-28 were invited to hang out, eat, talk, and play games all night long. He often asked some of his high-end clients to come in and give talks to the younger guys.

Simon had come a long way since those first days, so he could empathize with Karleigh. Becoming a business owner was no easy task. You had to have grit and determination to make it in this industry. Simon's first customers were the neighborhood kids. Most of them couldn't afford to pay for the haircuts they received. Some of the kids offered a few dollars when they could. The neighborhood was poor and blighted back then, but it had started to come up in the past few years.

New stores and offices opened in the area. Buildings from the past were being refurbished and brought back to life. New homes were being built, and the community was coming together. Rochelle Park was thriving like it used to in the past. Unfortunately, there were still a few stragglers from back in the day hanging around. People had to continue to remain cautious in certain areas.

"Simon!" Roxanne yelled his name from the front door. "Seriously, how much longer will that construction next door continue? My clients are having to park in the other parking lot, a block away, and walk over here." She rolled her eyes and dropped her large handbag into the barber chair closest to the front door. Roxanne always seemed to complain about something.

"Roxanne, what do you want me to do? Go over there and lend a hand to make the renovations go faster. My clients aren't happy, either." Simon spun in his chair to face her.

"For real, Simon," Marquez started. "Her construction crew is taking up all of the parking spaces, and then, they leave the dumpster full at night. I mean, she cute and all, but she is getting on our nerves. When will she be finished?"

Simon understood that the others were just as frustrated. Aside from the parking spaces being taken, the workers would leave debris all around the building. Tyrel got a flat tire from a nail just last week. Simon had to go over there and talk to her soon.

"OK! I'll go talk to her."

*****

Karleigh had been working day and night on preparing her salon. Her contractors had to nearly gut the entire space and rebuild it. Along with the electrical issues, they also found other problems with the plumbing. The owners of the building offered to pay for everything that needed repair behind the walls and beneath the floor, but Karleigh would be responsible for everything else.

The renovation costs were adding up to numbers that Karleigh just couldn't meet. She had to cut back on some of the things she really wanted to do. Instead of new carpet in the waiting area, she opted for a nice, cheap rug. She had ordered some comfortable chairs for the lobby but had to return them for something more economical. And, instead, of hiring professional painters, she enlisted her sister Poe to help.

Nothing was going the way she had pictured. Yet, she continued to thank God for all that she did have. The salon might not look as upscale as she wanted it to, but she still had a salon, and that was something to be grateful for.

She also felt terrible for Simon and his barbershop. They had to listen to the constant racket all day for the past three weeks. She knew she was getting on his nerves by the way he would briefly scowl instead of smile at her when their paths crossed. To her defense, Karleigh didn't know the space would need that much work.

Trying to switch her focus, she started reminiscing about when she first told her parents she wanted to go to cosmetology school. They had not been thrilled with her choice. Instead, they gently pushed her toward something more stable and traditional. She submitted to their wishes and went to college, earning a business degree. After graduation, she worked in corporate America for three years before she burned and crashed. She wasn't meeting her performance goals, no matter how hard she worked. She just didn't have a passion for the work she was doing.

Karleigh became withdrawn from family and friends. She stopped caring about herself and the people around her. Her daily routine included arriving to work late and leaving early. She was doing the bare minimum required for her job and secretly wished they would just terminate her. It was her sister, Karmyn, who snapped her out of her self-imposed funk.

Karmyn was the first to notice Karleigh's change in behavior. She staged an intervention and dragged her older sister into the spa for a relaxation makeover. During that time, Karmyn was able to find out that her sister needed to remember what made her happy. Karleigh had forgotten her passion for beauty and style until she sat in the stylist chair.

After the spa day with her sister, Karleigh immediately knew what she needed to do. The next week, Karleigh submitted her two-week notice to Human Resources and enrolled in cosmetology school. With help from her sister and working part-time at a restaurant, she was able to financially stay above water.

Her parents finally understood her decision and respected her chasing after her dreams. Something they never did. As a child, she did as she was told, but as a woman, her parents admired her independence. More than once, her mother and father had apologized to all the sisters about pushing them into specific careers. Only Kyna followed their laid-out path and enjoyed her life as an obstetrics nurse.

Karleigh started her beauty career at the Majesty Hair Salon right out of cosmetology school, then spent the last two years as a stylist at the Mane Event. The owner, Ms. Carter, was an older woman but tended to focus on the materialistic side of her craft. She was really into her "girls," as she often referred to her stylists, building a younger and trendier clientele. Karleigh's older clients were usually met with attitude and borderline disrespect. That was another reason she had to open her own place. A salon where everyone was welcomed.

Karmyn was pushed to become an engineer, but her life did a 180-degree turn when she married and then divorced, NFL star quarterback Vincent Gallagher. During their brief marriage, she fell in love with fitness and helping children and women achieve their fitness goals. Creating healthy lifestyles was her new passion. After the divorce, she opened her own fitness studio and gym. She returned to school and received a degree as a dietician. Her clients included neighborhood residents to professional athletes.

Poe was always rebellious. First, with her name, and then, with her career. She received a bachelor's degree in marketing and a master's degree in business administration but never had a career after college. She was still trying to find herself when she met a real estate agent. Poe loved everything about houses and helping people find their homes; thus, the real estate agent was born.

Karleigh was kneeling, inspecting some floor tiles when she heard a huge crash. She jumped up too fast and turned around quickly, losing her balance and tumbling over into the arms of Simon.

"I've heard of falling for a man, but I didn't think it was literal," Simon joked.

Karleigh attempted to stand and remove herself from his embrace. His touch caused a warming sensation to spread up her arm. A feeling that she had never felt before, and one that was not wanted. She pulled away with a little too much force.

"Why are you here, Simon?" Karleigh questioned him with attitude and sarcasm.

"What did I do to you?" Simon asked.

"Nothing," Karleigh closed her eyes and took a deep breath. "I'm sorry. I'm just not in a great mood today. I thought I would be open by now."

"That's what I came over to talk to you about. How much longer do you think this renovation will take?"

"Hopefully, they will have everything wrapped up by the end of the weekend. Then I'll need to come in and finish a few things." She looked around at all the workers, tarp-covered some of the furnishings that had been delivered. The amount of work she still had left to do overwhelmed her. She dropped her shoulders and sighed.

"Simon, did you have this much trouble when you opened your first store?" she asked.

Karleigh wasn't sure why she asked him that question. They hadn't said more than *hello* and *goodbye* in passing since they met. He was a fellow business owner in the beauty field, and she was looking for assurance that all of this would be worth it in the end.

"Well, when I first opened, it was a total dump. I didn't have the money to do a renovation. All of my barber chairs were donated or salvaged from back alleys."

Karleigh nodded her head for Simon to follow her. She walked toward the back of the salon, toward her office, the only room that didn't need to be demolished. Simon closed the door behind him.

"It's a little quieter in here," she explained. "So, in the end, all of this will be worth it? I think I'm letting my nerves get the best of me. I want so much to be successful." The room was quiet. For a quick second, Karleigh had forgotten Simon was there. Then she remembered to ask, "Why did you come over here?"

Jamming his hands into his pockets, "I was thinking about closing my shop while you renovate. My clients have been complaining."

Karleigh knew the noise was bothering him, but she didn't want him to lose business, either. Her renovations should have been aesthetic and should not have taken this long.

"I'm sorry, I didn't mean for you to lose business," she apologized.

"I'm not losing business. I can work from another location. I just think, maybe, it would be easier for my clients."

Karleigh looked at this situation in two different ways. He was making it known that she was bothering his business, or he was looking out for his clients, and that was excellent customer service. She decided to go with the latter, not wanting to think the worst of Simon. She had an idea, but before she could voice it aloud, Simon started speaking.

"You know, it looks like most of the work is finished out there. When do you start painting the walls?

Karleigh wasn't sure where this was going. "Actually, I was going to start painting tonight. I think one of my sisters is coming over to help."

"Great! I will just go change clothes and come help you," Simon was already reaching for the door.

"Wait! I didn't invite you to stay or help."

"Yes, you did. You want this place ready for your grand opening, and I have nothing I would rather do than to help you," Simon said with the wink of an eye and was gone.

Chapter 5

Karleigh was still shocked when Simon returned wearing a pair of well-faded denim jeans and a t-shirt that said Sharper Image Annual Picnic. She couldn't believe that he intended to help her paint the walls. The one question that kept coming back to her mind was, *Why?*

Why would he want to sweat all night, unless he had some type of ulterior motive? What was in it for him? No man would just offer physical labor unless he wanted something. Karleigh decided to keep her eyes and ears open to figuring out what his intention was.

"You were serious?" she asked when he entered.

"As a heart attack. I see the crew has gone for the evening."

"Yeah, it's just you and me until Poe shows up."

"Your sister's name is Poe?"

"No, it's Kaleigh. She hates her K name, so she goes by Poe. It's a long story, don't ask." Karleigh laughed, remembering when Poe gave everyone the silent treatment if they didn't address her as such. It lasted for over six weeks.

"Well, tell me where to find the brushes and paint, and I can get started."

Right! That's what he was there for. Karleigh showed him where all the supplies were and offered him a bottle of water. She had some work to finish up in her office but promised she would be out to help in under an hour.

She needed some time away from him to get herself together. Simon Sharpe was a handsome man, and if she didn't get herself together, she would look like an infatuated teenager in front of him. The perfect buffer would be Poe. Karleigh pulled out her cell phone to call her sister. If Poe were there, she would be able to focus on the painting, and not the man.

Karleigh tried five times to get Poe on the phone, leaving a message each time. She also sent two text messages. She had been in her office, stalling for 40 minutes. It was time for Karleigh to put on her big girl pants and face Simon. She finally gathered the courage to leave her office, mentally preparing to be alone with Simon.

"There you are, I really thought you were going to hide in your office all night and make us do all of the work," Simon said.

She had not expected to see Poe and another gentleman. They were all working hard at painting, along with Simon. She had no idea anyone else was in the salon. How had she not heard them enter?

Karleigh marched over to her sister, grabbing her arm to get her attention. Through clenched teeth, she asked, "I have been calling you. When did you get here?" Karleigh smiled over at Simon, then returned her scowl back to her sister.

"I've been here for about an hour. Simon said you were busy, so I thought I would just get started. My phone battery is dead. I just started charging it," Poe explained, pointing to her phone being charged against the wall.

Simon reclaimed her attention, "Karleigh, this is my frat brother, Nick." He tapped Nick on the shoulder to get his attention. Nick was wearing headphones and seemed to be in another world while he painted. "Nick, this is Karleigh."

Nick turned to say hi, but did a double-take, putting his brush down he approached Karleigh. "Simon, you didn't tell me your neighbor was gorgeous. Just like her sister," Nick flashed his $10,000 smile. "It is a pleasure to meet you. I would shake your hand, but Simon has me in here slaving for you. And, now I understand why."

Karleigh returned Nick's smile with one of her own. He was handsome, with young schoolboy features. Nick clearly was not the type to do manual labor. "So, Nick, what do you do for a living? I'm sure painting is not it."

"Mon Cherie, I do believe you have insulted me. I put in many hours painting in college. I had to earn money somehow. But, to answer your question, I'm an attorney."

"Yeah, he represents Tremaine Reed, the basketball player, and Skip Parker, the new safety for the Detroit Lions," Poe interjected.

"Well, Nick, you must be very good at your job. Thank you for accepting Simon's invitation to help." Karleigh looked around, trying to figure out where to start. There was only one paintbrush remaining, but no paint pans.

"Hey, you can share with me and start on this wall," Simon said, pointing to the walls where the new shampoo bowls would be installed later.

Just her luck, she would have to share the paint with Simon. He already had her thinking of him at the most inopportune times, and now she would have to work next to him, watching his biceps flex, while he moved the paintbrush up and down. Karleigh shook her head to remove the crazy thoughts from her mind.

For the next few hours, they all worked together in near silence. Nick had his headphones on and bobbed his head while painting the walls in the lobby. Poe was working on the left side of the salon, opposite where she and Simon were. There was the faint sound of the radio coming from Karleigh's office that could be heard. They all worked well together without having to say much.

"I'm hungry. Did no one think to order food," Poe complained.

"What time is it? What's open this late?" Simon asked.

"I'm sure a pizza place is still open. Let's get delivery. Everyone okay with pepperoni?" Nick replied.

"Pizza and hot wings. The hotter, the better," Poe said.

The pizza arrived 30 minutes after ordering, and the foursome retreated to Karleigh's office. Poe sat in the corner, on the floor with a plate of hot wings and two slices of pizza. Nick stood in the doorway, holding his plate of pizza. Simon and Karleigh shared her desk.

"So, Karleigh," Nick asked while shoving a slice of pizza in his mouth. "What made you want to own a salon?"

She didn't need time to think about it. "I always wanted to control my own fate. Having my own business is a part of that. And hair care is my passion. What about you? Why law?"

Simon jumped in to answer, "Nick loves the money, and with the money, come the girls."

Nick threw a balled-up paper napkin at Simon's head. "With all honesty, I admired a man named Mr. Coleman growing up. He was an attorney that worked on behalf of the little guy. He rarely charged people what his service was worth because he believed everyone needed representation."

Poe had just finished off her plate of wings when she asked, "Are you talking about Mr. Fred Coleman? I sold him his retirement home. That's a great guy."

Karleigh was fascinated by the easy camaraderie they had with one another. Until a few weeks ago, she had never heard of Simon Sharpe or Attorney Nicholas Butler. Both men were very successful, yet they were sitting on the floor, covered in paint dust, eating pizza, and talking like they had known one another for years.

"What about you, Simon? Why did you become a barber?" Karleigh asked.

*****

Simon had to answer this question several times over the years. He had gone from the business world's boy wonder in technology to the owner of a few barbershops. A few of his colleagues in business called him foolish for wanting to return home and become a barber. For Simon, he had no other choice, it was his legacy.

He watched Nick give him a look that said, *"Are you going to tell the truth or lie like all of the other interviews?"*

After giving it some thought, Simon decided to tell the partial truth. "I gave up a lucrative business position to come home and do what was right." He finally answered.

"And what was that? What was right?" Poe asked.

"I felt stifled in corporate America. I felt like a robot. I wanted to do more, I wanted my life to have meaning."

"So, being a barber gives your life meaning?" Karleigh asked.

The only person that knew the full truth was Nick and his grandfather. He looked around the room and felt a sense of peace, knowing that the people in the room wouldn't judge him. "My grandfather was a barber. He had a barbershop for years on the other side of town. Before he died, he lost his shop to some type of corporate shenanigans. He never recovered from losing everything and died a few months later. I promised him that I wouldn't let his legacy die. My father never wanted to be a barber, but growing up, it was all I knew." Simon looked away from Karleigh's caring eyes. If he wasn't careful, he might fall in too deep.

Trying to lighten the mood just a little, he continued, "I also enjoyed being in this community, giving back to those less fortunate, and showing the youth there are other ways to be successful than playing sports or becoming a doctor or a lawyer." He looked to Nick, "no offense."

Nick threw his hands in the air. "None taken," he replied.

"Very admirable," Karleigh responded.

"Yeah, Simon here is a real boy scout," Nick said while wiping his hands on a napkin and cleaning up his area. "Ladies, it has been a pleasure. But, I need to get out of here. Karleigh, I wish you all the best."

"Thanks, Nick," Karleigh replied.

"Hey, Nick, let me walk you to the door." Simon stood and gathered all their discarded food and plates. "I'll take the trash out to the dumpster with me."

Simon needed to know he wasn't going crazy. He had only known Karleigh for a few weeks and, yet, she was evoking strange emotions and feelings of forever within him. He gathered all of the trash from the office and put it in a bag and followed Nick outside.

"Nick, help me. Say something that will make me come to my senses," Simon half-heartedly joked.

"I can't. Karleigh is cool, and so is her sister. I could see you with someone like her."

"What? Am I dreaming? Not the 'bachelor for life, and everyone else is a sucka.' Those were your words, right?" Simon asked

"Yeah, I might have said that a time or two, but it never applied to you. Simon, you have always been the settling down type." Nick paused. "I never thought you would be the love and leave type."

Simon thought about his friend's words. Nick was right; he wasn't that type of man. Simon knew the first time he met Karleigh that she was special. Sure, she was beautiful and smart, but she had other qualities that Simon was learning about her.

"Simon, go in there and make sure they get home safely. Then, let fate take its course." Getting into his vehicle, he said: "And, hopefully, fate doesn't have me painting anymore."

Simon stood in the parking lot for a few minutes after Nick left. Nick knew him better than anyone. And if Nick was saying go for it, then he probably should. Simon was nervous about asking Karleigh on a date. Especially in front of her sister.

He returned to the salon and caught the end of the sisters' conversation.

"Sure, he's nice and attractive, but this salon is my first priority. I can't think about him right now." Karleigh said.

"But, if he asks, will you say yes?" Poe asked.

"Doubt it. I need to focus on this place. Priorities sister, priorities."

That put a damper on Simon's spirits, but that wasn't the end of it. Simon was no quitter. He had to figure out how to get her to say yes.

Chapter 6

Simon re-entered Karleigh's office with an idea of how he could spend more time with her. He just needed to get Poe to leave. With a stroke of luck, his opening came when Poe stood and gave a long yawn and stretch.

"Well, good people. This has been fun." Turning to Karleigh, Poe said, "I'll be back tomorrow night to finish up and help you with anything else. Sister, try to get some rest, okay?"

"Thanks, Poe. Love ya," Karleigh stood to give her sister hug. After their embrace, Poe gave Simon a look that he couldn't immediately decipher. It was a stern look and mixed with humor.

"Let me walk you to your car," Simon offered Poe. "Karleigh, I'll be right back."

Once outside, in the parking lot, Poe abruptly stopped and turned to Simon. "Listen, I like you. But, my sister is not to be messed with. Do you understand?" She paused before continuing, "I know people who have a particular set of skills. You get my drift?"

Simon laughed at her reference to the movie *Taken*. "What are you talking about? I'm just one business owner helping a fellow new business owner." Simon smiled, but Poe didn't lighten up.

Poe frowned. "It's in your eyes. Everything you are thinking can be seen in your eyes. And I'm watching you." Poe took her two fingers and pointed from her eyes to his.

Simon couldn't help but continue to laugh. Her antics were comical, but he knew she was serious. He stopped laughing and opened her car door. Chivalry wasn't dead.

"Thanks for walking me to my car, but make sure your intentions with my sister are honorable. I'm serious, I know people." Poe got in her car and sped away.

Simon was shaking his head when he came back to Karleigh. "Your sister is funny," he told Karleigh.

"Did she give you the 'I know people' spill?"

"Yeah. I take it she does that often."

"Only when she thinks she needs to. She is protective of her sisters like that. She's harmless, ignore her." Karleigh went into the restroom and closed the door.

Simon had to ask himself why he was interested in Karleigh? He hadn't had any genuine interest like this in a woman in years. Sure, he had gone on dates, but he hadn't wanted to get involved with those women.

With Karleigh, he could see a future. She was nothing like the women he had dated in the past. She was the marrying kind.

Poe said she could see it in his eyes. What exactly could she see? Could Karleigh see it, also? Was he that transparent? He did want to get to know her better. Was that what Poe was able to see in his eyes? They were going to be neighbors in business for possibly years to come. So, getting to know her was a natural thing, Simon kept telling himself.

Karleigh returned from the restroom and went right back to work on painting the trim work. She was determined to do as much by herself as she could. She had been going nonstop since earlier in the day. He understood why Poe told her to get some rest.

"Karleigh, you know you can finish this up tomorrow. It's already pretty late."

"Why put off until tomorrow what can be done today?" she looked over her shoulder to see where he was. "You don't have to stay. I'll be fine for another hour or so."

"There is no way I'm leaving you alone at this hour."

"Well, I'm not leaving just yet. If you are intent on staying, grab a brush, or just keep me company. Tell me something about yourself."

Simon inwardly smiled. She had just given him the opening he needed. "Well, I grew up not too far from here."

"Any siblings?" She asked.

Simon hesitated to answer. He rarely talked about himself to anyone. Outside of his family and Nick, no one knew he had a sister. But, Karleigh was so easy to talk to, that he didn't think twice about telling her.

"Yeah, I had a sister."

Karleigh turned to him and stopped painting. "*Had* a sister?"

"Yeah, she died a few years ago." Simon had to clear his throat. He hadn't told anyone this in so long, he forgot how emotional he got thinking about her. Quickly changing the direction of the conversation, he asked. "So, is it only the four of you sisters?"

He saw the look that Karleigh gave to him. She was going to let him change the subject this time. "Yeah, my mom wanted to give my father a boy, but after Kyna was born, my dad said his heart was full."

Simon could see the love she had for her family. It showed brightly in her eyes. He often wished he had a larger family. Brothers to play football or cousins to go fishing with. His parents were great, and his grandparents were the best. His sister came along when he was 15-years-old.

"How much more are you going to work on tonight?" Simon asked.

"Not sure. I know I want to finish this section and the trim work. Tomorrow, the shampoo bowls arrive, and I want to install them and the overhead cabinets."

"Who's doing your installation?"

"I have a company coming in to install all of the plumbing, sinks, and things, but I am planning to install the cabinetry by myself."

Simon thought she was really unbelievable. He didn't know many women like her, and that was one reason he had to get to know her better. He wanted to learn more about a woman who was willing to do it all to see her dreams come true.

"How about, after you finish this section, we call it a night, and I come back in the morning to assist you with your cabinets and anything else. I am pretty handy."

Simon felt like she was about to decline his offer, so before she could speak, he started again, "I will even bring breakfast. Donuts and juice from Moore's Bakery?"

"How can I resist free labor and donuts? I plan to be here by 9 A.M."

"9 A.M? Are you crazy? It's 3 A.M. now. When will you get some sleep?

"I only need a few hours. Adrenaline is better than coffee."

"I'll make a deal with you. Let's meet at noon, and I will bring extra helping hands." He paused to give her a chance to think it over. "We can do all of the work in less time. It's a win-win."

*****

Karleigh was clueless as to why Simon was offering to help her. He was doing more than she thought necessary. Yet, he was still there and still offering to help her. Then, she thought about something Poe said before she left…maybe Simon was interested in her.

Men like Nick and Simon weren't interested in plain-Jane women like her. She was merely a small business owner trying to get started. According to Kyna, he was some rich guy, probably getting his kicks off by taking pity on her. He would go home to his fancy condo downtown or mansion in the suburbs, and she went back to a small house on the east-side.

She thought more about his offer and motivation. On the one hand, she wanted to accept his offer. That would free up some time and money, both of which she had none. On the other hand, she didn't want to seem like a damsel in distress. She was perfectly capable of taking care of her salon and doing the work herself.

Weighing the options, she decided she would be a fool if she didn't accept his offer. Whether she liked it or not, she needed help. Trying to be a superwoman was only making her tired and cranky.

"You have a deal. Let me finish the trim, and I'm done for the night," she announced and went back to painting.

"Great! I'll just rinse out these brushes while I wait." He cleaned the area where Poe and Nick had been working, then collected the brushes and disappeared to the laundry area.

Karleigh was trying to keep her focus on painting, but her mind kept drifting back to Simon. He was gorgeous, and she just didn't attract gorgeous, successful businessmen. He had to want something else.

She finally finished the trim work, if that was what you would call it. The section would be under the new shampoo bowls, so she didn't mind that they weren't perfect. The plumbing guys would be bringing her sinks in the morning, and the remainder of the styling stations were being delivered in the afternoon. With Simon's help, her salon would be ready on time for the grand opening.

They worked well together. Within an hour, Simon and Karleigh had finished cleaning everything and were walking out of the building.

"Simon, thanks for everything. I'm not quite sure why you are doing this for me, but I do appreciate it." Karleigh didn't expect Simon to hug her, but he did. Instead of snatching away, she leaned into his hug and lingered a second longer than she should have.

"Karleigh, whenever you need help, just ask. I want to think we are fast becoming friends. I am a great resource if you ever need one and an overall great friend."

She pondered those words for a few seconds before getting into her car. "Well, then, I'm glad we are friends. Goodnight, Simon. See ya tomorrow with my donuts." She smiled before allowing him to close her car door.

She waited for him to get into his car, and together, they left the parking lot headed in different directions. Karleigh wondered where he lived? She thought he looked like the type to live in a fancy downtown apartment with a doorman. This was the second time she was thinking about where Simon lived.

Karleigh was aware of his VIP clientele, but often wondered why he made the quaint little neighborhood his barbershop headquarters. He could afford to have his barbershops in the more affluent areas, yet he preferred to work from the location in an up and coming area.

Her mind kept drifting to images and ideas of Simon. She wanted to think of something, anything else. She needed to talk to a sister, any sister.

At this hour, only Kyna would be awake. She was a nurse who worked crazy hours, mostly overnight.

The phone rang three times before Kyna's bubbly voice answered.

"Hey, sister. I heard you, and Simon Sharpe are getting cozy."

"Who told you that?" Karleigh said, with too much squeal to her voice. In a calmer tone, she said, "Why did I ask? I know it was Poe."

"Yeah, she called when she left you guys alone. She figured you would call me on your way home." Karleigh usually talked to a sister while she drove home from long trips or while in traffic.

"Well, she was wrong. We weren't getting cozy or anything. Her spidey-senses were all wrong this time."

"I don't think so. Poe told me that Simon was staring at you in awe, like a boy who wanted to ask the prettiest girl in school to prom. What's up with that?" Now Karleigh was getting annoyed. Poe always thought she could tell what others were thinking by watching their eyes. Like she was some kind of psychic.

"Kyna, stop believing everything Poe tells you. I just wanted to talk to you on my way home and tell you about the progress we made at the salon."

"So, talk. I'm all ears."

Being the baby of the family, Kyna often felt like she was being left out of conversations with her sisters. She would follow them around and listen to their conversations with their friends. They used to think she was just nosy and in their business all the time, but in college, they finally figured out they had left her behind.

Kyna started acting differently after Karmyn left for college. She didn't act out like some kids did to get attention. Instead, she withdrew from her sisters. When they would call home, Kyna never had time to talk to them. Karleigh came home to visit once and found her sister balled up in a corner crying.

Karleigh couldn't leave her like that, and they talked all night until Kyna finally came around and told the truth. All she wanted was to have her sisters home. That night, Karleigh was supposed to return to school, but instead, Karmyn drove home from her campus, which was three hours away, and Poe joined them by phone. The four sisters had been close ever

since. The sisters rarely went a day without communicating with each other in some way.

Kyna was the listener of the sisters, always available to listen and only offer her opinion when asked. She was the one person whom everyone went to in their time of need. Not that she would do anything special, she just allowed you to talk.

They talked on the phone until Karleigh made it home and had entered her house. Karleigh was exhausted and laid across her bed, fully dressed. She hadn't realized how much rest her body was screaming for. She wanted to take a shower and slip under the sheets. Instead, she fell asleep right where she laid.

Chapter 7

The next morning, Karleigh didn't awake until her alarm clock blared at 10 A.M. She was thankful that she made that deal with Simon. She doubted very seriously that she would have been able to wake up any earlier. Her body felt heavy as she rolled from her bed, still fully dressed, and dragged herself into the bathroom.

The reflection in the mirror was horrendous. Karleigh felt like an extra from the set of the TV show, The Walking Dead. There was no way she was meeting with Simon looking as she did. Karleigh quickly jumped in the shower and washed her hair.

There wasn't much she could do about the bags under her eyes or the redness. She didn't wear too much make-up, so she tried to camouflage any weariness with a little mascara and added lip gloss to draw attention to her lips.

She was supposed to meet Simon at the salon at noon, but she couldn't help making a stop at Starbucks to get them both some coffee. He had to be just as tired as she was. Karleigh arrived 15 minutes after noon and was shocked at what she saw.

"What is all of this?" she asked Simon.

"This is the Calvary," Simon winked at her. "You know my barbers Marquez and Tyrel. The other two guys are my fraternity brothers. That's Kendrick and Houston." All four men tipped their heads to Karleigh in greeting.

"Well, I hadn't expected this," she mumbled under her breath. The two coffees she had in her hands wouldn't be enough. She decided if they would do this for her, she could, at the very least, get them all coffee. She took their orders and quickly headed to Java Times, which was closer.

Simon started barking orders as soon as Karleigh returned. The guys moved with precision, asking questions when needed and never making a decision that she was not involved in. Tyrel went back and forth between the barbershop and the salon. It was a workday for him, and he had clients to take care of. Karleigh had found it strange that Marquez didn't seem to ever have any clients.

The plumbing team arrived an hour later, but the shampoo bowls had not. Karleigh immediately contacted the company, only to discover they had the wrong delivery date. She wanted to cry, it seemed that Murphy's Law was taking over her life.

Instead of staying out front with the guys, she hid in her office. She was trying to come up with a solution, but nothing was coming to mind. To have the plumbers come back would cost money she didn't have. Simon found her sitting at her desk, crying her eyes out.

"Hey, Karleigh, what's wrong?" he asked, concerned.

She told him about the shampoo bowls not arriving for another four days.

Between sobs, she said, "It seems like when it rains, it really pours. I must have been out of my mind to want to start my own business."

Simon wanted to console her. He walked behind her desk and gently rubbed her back to offer some comfort. "You were unhappy where you were. Sure, you could still be at the other salon working for other people. But, you know, like I do, that working for yourself is a completely different feeling. When you realize your passion, you won't be happy until you fulfill it."

She knew he was right. Her passion for beauty was why she was willing to endure everything that was happening. Being a business owner came with the good and the bad. Right now, the bad was in not knowing what to do about the shampoo bowls.

Simon must have read her mind when he asked, "Where are the bowls? Where did you order them from?"

Karleigh looked up and into his eyes before answering, "From the Elm St. Liquidators on the other side of town."

"I will go get the bowls myself, and while the guys are still around, we can install them for you."

This was too much for Karleigh to accept. Here was this guy she barely talked to in passing, offering all this help after one, late-night, impromptu paint party. "Simon, I can't keep depending on you to bail me out of trouble. I appreciate the offer, but I can't accept it."

Simon dropped down to be eye level with Karleigh while she sat at her desk. "Karleigh, the way I see it, you don't have a choice. You want this place to be perfect, and I want to help you."

"That's just it, why do you want to help me? I have caused nothing but trouble since I got here. Yet, you still want to spend your time putting in manual labor for me. What do you want from me, Simon?"

"Have a meal with me. Any meal. I like you, Karleigh, and I want you to know I'm a good guy."

Karleigh thought about his offer. She didn't need the headache of a man in her life right now, but Simon would be a part of her life no matter what. He worked next door, and she wouldn't be able to avoid him forever.

Maybe if she offered a ridiculous time in the morning, he would change his mind.

"Any meal? Okay, breakfast it is. 7 A.M., tomorrow," she thought he would balk at the time, but instead, he smiled and agreed. Simon was out of the door before she could come up with a reason to decline or to tell the truth and say she was just joking. Now she was stuck with having to go to breakfast with him.

Simon and his fraternity brother, Houston, left to pick up the shampoo bowls, and Karleigh felt like she accepted a date with the devil.

*****

Simon swiftly grabbed Houston, and they jumped into Houston's Dodge pick-up truck. It also helped that Houston was a big, bulky, linebacker-built guy. He probably bench-pressed 400 pounds without sweating. Simon stood over 6 feet tall and appeared small next to his fraternity brother.

"Bro! Come on, man, what's the deal between you and Karleigh?" Houston asked.

"What makes you think there is something between us?" Simon couldn't help but smile.

"Really? Playing coy is not who you are. I see how you watch her. And, to top it all off, you got me over here doing manual labor, knowing you will owe me big for this."

Simon knew he was right. Houston was a landscaper who rarely missed a day of work. But, when he did, it was because someone he cared about needed him. So, to lie to him would be futile.

"She is special. I know I just met her, but I can feel an attraction like none other with her. Have you ever felt this way?"

"Yeah. When I met Nikki, she said one word to me, and I was a goner."

"I remember that. You were sitting in her seat at the football game. She looked at you, and then, at her ticket, then, at you again. Then, she said, 'move.'" Simon laughed at the memory.

"Yeah, well, she may have been a little rough around the edges, but she has mellowed out since then. I knew I would marry her that day."

"Whoa, Bro! Slow down. No one said anything about getting married. I'm just saying I like her and I want to be there for her. One small-business owner helping another."

"Yeah, ok," Houston said, not believing a word Simon was saying. "So, have you two been on a date yet?"

"Breakfast, 7 A.M." Simon laughed because he knew she was trying to get him to back out on the deal.

"If you are really interested in her, make sure to show up and show out. One up her every time. If she wants to meet at 7 A.M., make sure you are early, and bring something special."

Simon thought about what Houston was telling him. He had to know something about women and relationships. Nikki and Houston had been married for 15 years and had three amazing children, all boys; Denver, who was eight years old, Chicago was five years old, and Memphis was two years old. Houston kept his family tradition by naming his boys after cities. He also had two younger brothers named Austin and Dallas.

When they arrived at the warehouse, they ran into another glitch. Karleigh had needed five shampoo bowls, and the liquidators only had four. The bowls she ordered were a deep metallic blue. Simon looked around for something comparable. The only other shampoo bowls he found were much more expensive than the ones Karleigh selected.

"Simon, what about these?" Houston found some bowls in a similar color scheme as the salon. They weren't porcelain, but a more expensive brushed stainless steel. Simon motioned for the manager to come over.

"Hey, are these available for sale?"

"Sure, they were a custom order, but the salon never came to pick them up. I could give them to you for 10% off the list price."

Simon calculated the cost in his head, and it was still significantly over her budget.

"Let me ask you this. What would you usually do with an order like this?"

"Typically, we would send them back to the manufacturer. But, this particular manufacturer doesn't take returns of custom orders. So, I guess we have to keep these until we sell them."

"Okay, let's make a deal. Give me these five bowls for the price of the porcelain bowls, and I will promise to replace all my barber chairs from only you in all of my barbershops within the next six months. As good faith, I will put down a deposit of $2,500 today."

Simon watched the manager calculate the commission in his head. He knew the deal was sealed when the manager gave him the Cheshire cat smile and motioned for his warehouse crew to load the truck.

"Simon, aren't you going to check with Karleigh first?"

"You said, go big or go home."

"I didn't actually say those words, but I guess this is going big," Houston slipped on his sunglasses and laughed while walking away.

Simon and Houston arrived back to the salon an hour later. Karleigh was talking on the phone and appeared upset. Simon thought it couldn't possibly be more bad news. He approached her and saw the tears in her eyes. She held up a finger indicating for him to wait a minute.

"Thank you so much. I love you." Karleigh spoke into the phone.

Simon's emotions immediately went into a spiral. He had no idea who she was talking to, but inwardly wished it was not another man. She had told him she wasn't seeing anyone. He had no reason not to believe her. Someone she loved had clearly upset her, and he wanted to know who and why.

"Is everything okay? Who was that?"

"I have no reason to tell you who I was having a private conversation with," Karleigh took a step away from Simon.

He had stepped in it again with her. Not wanting to anger her further and still having to tell her about the shampoo bowls, Simon figured he had to tread lightly with her.

"Karleigh, I apologize. You seemed upset and ... I guess I overstepped."

"Yes, you did."

"Well, I have to tell you about the liquidators. It seems they did not have the shampoo bowls you selected, or rather they didn't have enough. So, I got you a deal on another type. I hope you approve. If not, I can return them."

Simon was not sure why he said he could return them. The manager had told him they were non-refundable because they were a custom order. If she decided she didn't want them, he would have to use them for himself.

Karleigh walked over to Houston's truck and watched him open a box. Her reaction was no indicator of what she was thinking. Simon fidgeted, waiting for her to respond. Even Houston was confused with her response or lack thereof.

For several seconds the men just looked back and forth from one to the other and then to Karleigh. A single tear escaped her eye, but Simon had no idea if that was a good thing or a bad thing.

"How much did you have to pay for me to get these?"

"I didn't have to pay anything," he said while reaching into his pocket to get her invoice. "Here is your invoice and receipt."

Karleigh grabbed the paper from Simon and reviewed the information. She then folded the invoice and placed it into her pants pocket. "Thank you for going to get them for me. But, I still don't have anyone to install them. The plumbers left."

Simon hated to see the defeated look on her face. If he had to watch YouTube videos and work all night, she would have her shampoo bowls installed.

"Karleigh? Simon? Did you forget what I do for a living?" Houston asked.

"You're a landscaper, not a plumber," Simon responded.

"Correct, but I also install irrigation systems, and some of them can get to be quite complex. A few years ago, I became certified as a plumber, and I keep my education up-to-date by trading services with a few friends. With everyone's help, I can have these installed in a few hours."

"I can't ask you to do that. You being here and what you have done all day was more than enough."

"Karleigh, I believe I volunteered my services," Houston winked at her. "Besides, my wife would kill me if she found out I didn't help you."

Simon laughed and turned to Karleigh, "Believe me, she might try it."

Chapter 8

By 5pm, the salon was all put together and only needed the loving decorative touch of her mother.

Karleigh's heart swelled when she surveyed the entire space. Everything looked just like her dreams. An emotional wave washed over her and, in her joy, came tears. Poe had been right, where there is a will, God will make a way.

Quickly wiping away her tears, Karleigh walked over to each of the guys and thanked them for all their hard work. Without them or Simon, she wouldn't have been able to get the place together as quickly as they did. Houston and Kendrick were leaving when Karmyn arrived.

Karmyn must have been coming from her gym because she was dressed in black leggings and a flimsy halter top emblazoned with her gym's logo over her bright pink sports bra. These days, that was Karmyn's attire of choice. She claimed it was brand marketing, but it seemed more like she was attention-seeking or too lazy to get dressed every day.

"It looks good in here, sister. You guys did a great job."

As Karmyn was looking around, Karleigh noticed Tyrel's reaction to her sister. Marquez took two fingers and tipped Tyrel's chin up to help him close his mouth. The scene was all too familiar and still funny. Karleigh envied that about her sister. She had a beautiful body and kept in shape by owning a successful fitness gym courtesy of ex-husband.

Karmyn was the adventurous sister. She was also the focused and driven one. If she wanted to do something, Karmyn went out of her way to do it. She would pull stunts like sneaking out of the house with Poe to get French fries in the middle of the night. She also had a knack for keeping the entire truth from people. If someone asked her a question, Karmyn would always have an answer that wasn't a lie but wasn't the whole truth, either.

In the past two years, Karleigh had spent a lot of time with Karmyn. They frequently had business meeting sleepovers and went on trips to entrepreneurship conferences. Karleigh learned more in the two years shadowing Karmyn than she had learned in all of her time in business school.

"All that's left now is for mom to come in and put her touch on everything," Karleigh said.

"Well, I think it looks great without mom's touch. Sister, I am so proud of you." Karmyn hugged her tightly. "So, what are the plans for the grand opening party?" she asked.

"You're having a grand opening party?" Simon asked.

Both sisters turned in his direction. Simon was just returning from dumping some trash in the back of the building.

"Simon, you remember my sister, Karmyn." The two shook hands before Karleigh continued. "I'm planning a huge block party style grand opening in two weeks." Karleigh watched his facial expressions change, and she quickly tried to address his concern.

"Don't worry, it's planned for a Sunday. Mr. Dorsey said you're not open on Sundays, so I can use the entire parking lot."

There was a collective sigh from Simon, Tyrel, and Marquez. The other two barbers had been standing nearby when Karleigh mentioned having a grand opening. She figured they would be concerned about the parking situation. But, she had taken them into consideration before planning her opening event.

*****

Simon thought about the benefits of her having a grand opening. He could get his shop involved to help her out and maybe draw up some business for himself.

"What does your block party consist of?" Simon asked.

"Well, for starters, I have a DJ coming and a bounce house for the kids. There will be a face painter and some vendors, friends of mine. My dad is bringing his huge grill over and providing free dogs and burgers for the children. Then, I'm planning to offer free quick hairstyles, and my esthetician will be providing free facials."

Simon first noticed how her eyes lit up when she started talking about the things she had planned. Then, he saw a little apprehension in her body language. He guessed she was nervous about everything and just wanted things to be perfect. "Do you mind if the Sharper Image participates? We can provide free haircuts, and if you want, donate the sodas and waters."

Tyrel started coughing at the word free while Marquez remained silent. Simon sent both of them a frown before returning his attention back to Karleigh. She first appeared confused, then, with a nudge from her sister, she smiled.

"Sure. The more, the merrier. I will see if I can add the free haircuts to the flyer. We have been doing a lot of promoting on social media, also. Feel free to add it to your events, as well."

Simon didn't realize he was holding his breath until she answered. He was positive this would be a good thing, and he would get to see Karleigh in her element. Seeing her do what she enjoyed gave him a funny feeling he wasn't able to describe.

"Excuse me, Simon," Tyrel interrupted. "Can I talk to you for a minute? Excuse us, ladies."

Tyrel practically dragged Simon by his collar outside, where the ladies couldn't hear him. Marquez followed behind them.

"Dude! Are you crazy? You just offered us up for free again!" Tyrel retorted.

"And, on a Sunday," Marquez added.

Simon hadn't thought about them at all. He figured he would be the one cutting hair. But, if they could be persuaded to participate, that may free up some of his time to watch Karleigh. He knew it was an inconvenience from Tyrel, but not Marquez. Marquez rarely did anything on the weekends.

"I'll cover the cost of your cuts. Just think about it," Simon pleaded.

"How do you know we're available on that Sunday?" Marquez asked.

"Oh, yeah. Are you two available?" Simon smugly asked.

"Just us two? What about Roxane? Are you going to ask her?" Tyrel said.

Simon knew he couldn't ask her. She was likely to become hostile. Roxanne had a temper; anything could set her off. Even her clients felt her wrath. The only time she was calm was when she was with her children.

"You know I'm not asking her." Simon dropped his head, attempting to look sorrowful, "You guys don't have to do it. I'll take care of it myself." Simon was resigned to handle as many cuts as he could. Once again, he had opened his mouth to offer something that he wasn't sure how he could deliver.

"You better be glad I like Karleigh. She's good people." Poking Simon in the chest with his index finger, Tyrel said, "You better not be playing with her."

Simon felt like he was being warned by a girl's big brother. First Poe with her threats, and now Tyrel. He watched both men walk away and couldn't help but wonder why he was doing all of this for a woman he just met? How serious was he about her?

He decided not to think about his why's anymore and returned to the salon. He found Karleigh and her sister in the back office chatting away. "I don't mean to interrupt ladies, but I'm going to head out. Do you need anything before I leave, Karleigh?"

"I think you and your friends have done enough. Thank you so much for the help," she said, standing to give him a hug before he left. She returned to her desk and said, "You were right when you said it would be faster if I had more hands. I don't know how to pay you back."

Once again, Simon was speaking before thinking, "You can go to dinner with me tonight."

"Dinner? Tonight? I thought we were meeting for breakfast?"

"We can still have breakfast in the morning."

"You should go, sister." Karmyn laughed, then directed her attention to Simon. "I bet she hasn't eaten since she got here."

"You know your sister well. She showed up at noon with a cup of coffee and hasn't slowed down since. This is the first time I have seen her sitting."

"You two know I can hear you, right? I'm sitting right here." Karleigh was clearly annoyed.

Simon turned his attention back to Karleigh, "It's nothing formal, there's a deli nearby with a killer corned beef sandwich. Karmyn, you're welcome to join us."

"Oh no, Simon. I don't do the whole third wheel thing. I was heading back to the gym, anyways." She gave her sister a quick hug. "You two have fun." Karmyn laughed as she left them alone.

Karleigh stared at Simon. He was starting to feel warm underneath her gaze. She didn't say anything for a few minutes. When she did speak, her voice was laced with unexpected venom.

"You have effectively made two of my sisters believe you are interested in more than friendship with me. Why?"

Simon stumbled for words to say. He hadn't set out to make her sisters believe anything. He admitted that he was attracted to her, but his wanting to help her came from the heart.

"I can't control what they think. To be honest with you, I just wanted to help you to get your renovations done faster. You were taking up more than half of the parking lot. Once I got to know you better, I found you fascinating. I want to be around you more often and talk to you."

"Simon, since we're being honest. I don't think it's a good idea for us to date. We have to work next door to each other every day. What if we have a bad breakup, then, what?"

"Whoa, Karleigh, I was just asking you to get a sandwich tonight. You already have us breaking up." He smiled at her when she looked horrified. "I just want to be your friend. Let's start there. No expectations."

Simon noticed Karleigh had a habit of blankly staring while trying to formulate a put-down or kiss-off response. "Sorry, Simon, it's just not a good time for me."

"What about breakfast in the morning?"

"About that. When I offered it, I was hoping you wouldn't accept it. No breakfast, either. But, thank you for everything today. I couldn't have done it without you and your friends." She gathered her bags to leave, then waited for him to lead out of her office. He didn't attempt to change her mind. There were some battles worth fighting and this wasn't one of them.

Chapter 9

Opening day had finally arrived. The final touches of décor were put in place. Everything was perfect when Karleigh finally headed home the night before the grand opening. The anxiety and excitement kept her awake through much of the night. When she was able to eventually drift off to sleep, it seemed her alarm clock began blaring. Operating on only a few hours of sleep, Karleigh excitedly prepared herself for her grand opening. The beginning of something that belonged only to her.

Her grand opening celebration was a community affair. She scheduled to have two bounce houses and face painting for the children. DJ Hard Rock was hired to play energetic music and keep the crowd entertained. There would be a couple of food trucks and a few other vendors. Serenity Salon and Spa would be providing free massages from their newly contracted masseuse and free facials. Simon and his barbers joined in and were offering free haircuts for children under twelve years old.

Karleigh opened her front door and stood on her porch, stopping to take a deep breath. Placing one hand over her heart and closing her eyes, she told God, 'thank you.' He was showing out in her life right now, and she needed to stop and give Him the glory.

On her drive into the salon, she suddenly felt a weird sense of anxiety wash over her. *"Stay positive, chick. Just stay positive,"* she told herself. Karleigh didn't want to have any negative thoughts. She drove the streets in her neighborhood and marveled at how beautiful the day was beginning. The radio was off, and she just listened to nature. The birds chirping calmed her nerves just a little, but in the back of her mind, she had a nagging feeling.

She pulled into the parking lot very slowly; she wanted to take in the atmosphere of her first day. Vendors would start arriving in a few hours, and she wanted to be prepared for them. Instead of the pride, she thought she would feel, she immediately had a feeling of dread. Then she saw the very thing she never expected to see.

The front window, the beautiful feature of her salon, the first thing she fell in love with when she visited the building six months ago, was shattered. The new curtains that her mother lovingly hung the night before were blowing in the wind. Karleigh felt like she was seeing things on a movie screen. None of it seemed real. She slowly exited her vehicle and walked toward her salon. So quickly, her dreams were being crushed.

She distantly heard Simon say to someone on the phone, "She's here now, let me call you back."

Trying to hold the tears at bay, Karleigh whispered, "Everything I worked for, all of the money I saved, gone." A single tear dropped from Karleigh's eye. She clutched the silver necklace that she had been waiting to wear for this very day. Her grandmother had given her the silver and pearl necklace before she passed away.

"Karleigh?" Simon said.

"Why would someone do this?" She turned to Simon, "How long have you been here?"

"I got here five minutes ago and found it like this. I already called the police."

The police…right. Karleigh hadn't even thought that far. All she could see was the destruction of her dream. "I need to see if anything was stolen." She started toward the building but was stopped by Simon.

"Let's wait for the police to get here. You don't want to destroy any evidence they might find."

He was right, again. What would Karleigh do if Simon had not been there? She would have screamed and cried. Instead, Karleigh slumped against the hood of her car and dropped her head into her hands. She felt the soothing caress of Simon rubbing her back. Strangely, she liked it, and it felt comforting and reassuring. She needed his support and was grateful he was there.

Since the night of the impromptu paint party, Simon had checked in on her progress and offered his labor by installing her cabinets. Last week, he and Tyrell stopped by with dinner, because Simon knew she hadn't eaten. He had been a friend when she hadn't realized she needed one, even after she shot him down for dinner and breakfast.

The police arrived and questioned her and Simon. They were looking around the salon while Karleigh and Simon waited in the parking lot. Jasmine, the esthetician, came a few minutes later.

"Hey, girlie. What happened?" Jasmine asked.

"Looks like someone smashed in the window and trashed the place." Karleigh's voice quivered. She was drawing from Simon's strength. She was thankful he was still there with her.

"Was anything stolen?" Jasmine asked.

"I don't… I don't…" Karleigh couldn't answer the question. The tears took over, and her voice wouldn't work. She leaned into Simon, who instinctively put his arm around her shoulder.

Simon spoke up and answered the question, "We don't think so. It appears whoever did this just tossed things on the floor and spray painted the walls."

The three of them waited in the parking lot until they received the go-ahead from the police to enter the salon.

*****

Simon was just as shocked as everyone else that Karleigh's salon would have been vandalized. Of all the businesses on their block, someone picked hers to destroy. There were jewelry shops and clothing boutiques on the same block, but someone chose a hair salon to vandalize. It didn't make sense.

The vandals had tossed all her hair products on the floor, spray-painted obscenities on her walls, and smashed her front picture window. Simon was relieved that the inside fixtures were still in tack, and none of the appliances were missing. This didn't look to be a random attack. For some strange reason, Simon thought Karleigh may have been targeted.

The police took statements and left to file their report when Karleigh's family arrived. Simon knew she was in good hands with her sisters, he didn't need to worry about her. However, he felt an impulse that he needed to stay and make sure Karleigh was going to be okay. But, with her sisters hovering around her, he retreated to his business sanctuary.

Simon had been in his office for about 10 minutes when Tyrel walked in.

"Yo, Simon. You see what happened next door? I ain't never seen Karleigh like that before."

"Like what? Are her sisters still with her?" He asked with a level of concern that he didn't want Tyrel to hear, but it was too late.

"She was crying, really breaking down. I think her parents were pulling up when I walked in." Tyrel went about preparing his station for the day. "You think our security cameras caught anything?"

Simon hit himself against the head. "Stupid! I forgot we had cameras. Let me call the monitoring company." After waiting on hold for over thirty minutes, he found out it would take another six hours to get the footage available for him and the police.

Wanting to share this information with Karleigh as soon as possible, he left the shop and walked toward the salon. He found the Hammond family holding hands in a circle and praying. He felt like he was prying on a private family moment, but they were standing in the open parking lot. He waited for the prayer to end before he approached the group.

Seeing Karleigh crying and visibly defeated at the situation, tore at Simon's heart. He hated to see bad things happen to good people. She was working hard to make her dreams come true, and someone tried to take that from her

"Hey, Karleigh, I have some information for you that I hope will help. I forgot I have security cameras at my shop," Simon pointed out the cameras

on the building and in the parking lot. "I called the monitoring company, and they're going to send a copy of the videos to the police."

Simon wasn't ready for Karleigh to launch herself into his arms. She almost toppled them over onto the pavement. He was shocked at her reaction but more surprised at his response to her. She tried to slip from his embrace, but he held on for a few seconds longer. He liked the smell of her hair and the feel of her body next to his. He finally released her when one of her sisters cleared her throat.

Even if her attitude toward him had softened, Simon had to be careful around Karleigh. She was causing him to feel things he hadn't felt for a woman in a long time. He liked her, wanted to date her, but he wasn't trying to fall in love with her. He had to mentally slap himself for that last thought. Where had the L-word come from?

"Thank you, Simon. I appreciate you doing that." Karleigh looked embarrassed at what she had done. He knew she hadn't intended to jump on him. She looked down at her feet for a second, then back up to him. He gave her a smile to ease the awkwardness that had occurred.

"How about I send my security guys over here today and install a system for you?"

She looked down, again, and fidgeted with her hands before whispering, "Simon, I can't afford a security system. I was hoping I wouldn't need one for at least another few months."

"Don't worry about it. I'll take care of it." The words were out of his mouth before he had a chance to think. Her parents and sisters were eyeing him suspiciously. It was too late for him to take the offer back.

"Absolutely not. I am determined to do this on my own. I hate that I had to take a loan from my parents, but I will not take any charity." She stared him in the eyes and silently dared him to say something else. He decided it was best to back down, especially in front of her family.

Instead of saying more about the security system, he placed his hands in his pockets and asked, "So are these your parents?"

Simon smiled at the way her eyes widened in surprise when she realized they were having this conversation in front of her parents and sisters. She sheepishly turned to them and introduced her parents to him.

Kyra Hammond was absolutely beautiful and could easily pass for a fifth sister. Their father, Kevin Hammond, was tall and towered over the women, but met Simon eye-to-eye at 6'5." It was apparent that Kevin worked out. He had the solid frame of a football linebacker.

"It's a pleasure to meet you, Mr. and Mrs. Hammond," he said, shaking each of their hands. Sensing another awkward moment, Simon turned back to Karleigh. "Well, I will get back to my shop. Let me know if you want the number to my security guys," he spun around and headed back to his shop.

Chapter 10

Romans 8:28. And we know that all things work together for good to them that love God, to those who are the called according to His purpose. (NKJV)

"Okay, sister, it seems like you and Simon Sharpe are pretty good friends," Karmyn teasingly said.

"Whatever, Karmyn," Karleigh rolled her eyes. "Let's just get in here and salvage as much as we can. The grand opening is in three hours."

"What?" The three sisters spoke at once.

"Karleigh, you can't be serious?" Kyna asked. "You aren't going to go forward with the opening?"

Karleigh was very serious. She had planned this day for far too long to let anyone stop her. She probably wouldn't be able to offer some of the free services like she had advertised since the products were damaged, but she could still have the other events and giveaways. The DJ was scheduled to arrive in two hours. Nevertheless, there was going to be a celebration.

She turned to her family, "I refuse to cry over spilled milk when we still have cookies and cake." She gave her family a fake smile that didn't quite reach her eyes and walked away.

"I guess that's the final answer. Let's get ready," Jasmine said and followed Karleigh into the salon.

For the next two hours, Karleigh, her family, and Jasmine cleaned the broken glass, scrubbed the walls, and put some semblance of order back to the salon. Together, they were able to clean all the spray paint from the mirrors and cover the remaining spray paint on the walls with the curtains that previously hung in the front window.

Mr. Hammond started the grill for the hot dogs and hamburgers, the DJ arrived on time and began setting up, and everything appeared to be working out. Karleigh was starting to get some of her excitement back. Her sisters went to the local copy store and made coupons for the services she couldn't perform. She appreciated how much her family really supported her.

At exactly 4:00 PM, the community started arriving. Children were getting balloon animals and face painting. The DJ had the crowd engage in a popular line dance. Most of the people in attendance hadn't realized the window to the salon was missing.

Simon and his barbers had finished haircuts early enough to partake in the festivities. Tyrel was trying to show Karmyn how to ballroom dance. He was shocked to find out she had two left feet. Marquez and Kevin Hammond knew each other from grade school and were catching up on the old days.

Despite everything that happened, the grand opening still turned out to be a success. Karleigh interacted with everyone who came by. She talked to teenage girls about quick and easy hairstyles, she gave an impromptu lecture on healthy hair care, and she taught an older gentleman how to roller set his wife's hair so she wouldn't have to come into the salon as often.

She had been so busy that she temporarily forgot about Simon. She wanted to make sure she expressed her appreciation before he went home. Looking around the parking lot, she couldn't find him. Had he left without saying anything? Karleigh was disappointed that he wouldn't at least say goodbye, and she was confused with the reaction she was having with him being gone.

"I bet you're looking for Simon," Kyna asked her before stuffing a hotdog in her face.

"What makes you think that?" Karleigh tried to feign indifference.

"Because you keep looking around and you have this sad little look," she mocked a sad face with a frown.

"I do not. And, don't let mom see you talking with your mouth full," Karleigh laughed and returned to her salon.

When she re-entered the salon, she found yet another surprise from Simon. He and his friend Nick had just finished scrubbing the remaining graffiti from the walls. The gesture was going to cause Karleigh to cry again. No one outside of family had done this much to see to her success. Simon turned to and gave her his most perfect smile. The smile that had her thinking crazy thoughts of marriage and kids.

*****

Nick arrived, at Simon's request, while the party outside was in full swing. Simon took him aside to show him the damage and talk to him alone. At least the door was left intact, and no of the fixtures were damaged.

"Someone really did a number in here," Nick said when he entered. "Does she have enemies?"

"I don't know, but that's what I wanted to talk to you about. Can you get one of your guys on this?" Simon asked.

Nick represented some of the wealthiest people in the city, having bodyguards and private investigators available was a necessary evil in his line of work.

"Well, I doubt very seriously this was random. The writing on the wall says 'Loser' and 'You won't win.' Looks very personal,"

Simon walked to the back of the salon and grabbed a bucket and some towels. He filled the bucket with hot, soapy water and tossed the towels at Nick.

"What's this for?" Nick asked.

"What do you think? Get to work," Simon laughed as he rolled up his sleeves.

"Really, Simon. If we weren't such good friends, I would tell you where to go," Nick laughed and removed his jacket.

Simon was laughing at something Nick was saying when Karleigh walked in. She had that look on her face again. The one that said, you are doing too much. "Hey, Ms. Hammond. It's the least I could do," Simon told her.

"I was blackmailed into helping," Nick joked.

Karleigh smiled at Nick's humor, and that caused a slight hitch in Simon's breathing. She was beautiful, even standing here, smiling on what could have been the worse day of her business life. Instead, she made the best of the day and kept going with the event like she planned. She had determination and grit, two characteristics that Simon liked.

"Karleigh, Nick, and I want to talk to you about the vandalism," Simon started. "We think this may have been personal."

Karleigh took a seat in one of the salon chairs. "Why would you think that?"

Simon walked over to her and grabbed her hand. Gently rubbing his thumb over the back of her hand, he wanted to make sure she knew she had his support. "The messaging was personal, and nothing was stolen."

He went on to tell her everything he and Nick had discussed. This time he asked her if she would be okay with using Nick's investigator guys to look into some things. Simon wasn't sure what to expect from the independent woman, but she accepted their assistance without a fight.

Simon was still holding her hand when Karleigh's sister Karmyn walked in.

"Am I interrupting something?" Karmyn directed her question to her sister but looked at Simon.

Karleigh snatched her hand away and jumped up from the chair. She couldn't go too far because Simon was blocking her way. He let her hand go but wasn't about to back down or move out of the way. He stood in place and intentionally made it difficult for Karleigh to go around him.

"Nothing at all, Karmyn," Simon said with slight agitation in his voice. "We were just finishing up in here." He never let his gaze leave Karleigh's face. He could tell she was becoming uncomfortable. Tough! He had been restless ever since he met her. He blocked her path for a few seconds more before moving aside and allowing her to pass by.

He stepped out of her way and sat in the styling chair Karleigh had just vacated. "Karmyn, have you met my friend, Nick," Simon asked.

The room became eerily silent as Karmyn and Nick stared at each other, challenging the other to speak first. Simon wasn't sure, but it appeared the two of them knew each other, and not on good terms.

"Yeah, I know him," Karmyn spat out. "I just came in here to check on you, Karleigh. I see you're fine. I'm out of here." She turned around and returned outside.

"What was that all about?" Karleigh asked Nick.

"Your sister and I have had some run-ins in our past," Nick answered.

"I take it she doesn't like you," Simon asked.

"Understatement. She hates me." Nick gathered his jacket and turned to Karleigh. "I'll have my guys look into things around here. I'll let you know if they find anything."

"Thanks, Nick," Simon and Karleigh spoke at once.

They watched Nick leave and then turned to each other with the same bewildered look. Realizing they were both clueless to what just happened between Karmyn and Nick, they laughed hysterically until Poe entered.

"What did I miss?" Poe asked.

*****

The sleek black limousine didn't seem to draw any attention from the partygoers. The Dorsey brothers watched from behind tinted windows. Neither said anything, just smiled at each other and asked the driver to continue away.

Chapter 11

Nick was sitting in Tyrel's barber chair, flipping through emails on his phone, hanging out after working hours. The other barbers had gone home for the evening. "What gives Simon?" Nick asked without lifting his head from the screen. "She's been up and running for four weeks now. When are you going to ask her out?"

"Say what?" Simon acted like he didn't hear his friend.

"Let's not play that game. You were supposed to ask her out weeks ago. What happened?"

Simon couldn't lie to Nick even if he tried. Nick would know he was lying, so Simon didn't bother. He wanted to tell his friend that he had attempted to ask her out…a few times…but she declined each time. A man could only take so many rejections. She had reverted to her monotone greetings in the parking lot.

"I asked, and she said no, so I cut my losses." Simon continued to sweep the hair from around his station.

"Nope, not the Simon Sharpe, I know. I know you are still feeling her."

"What makes you think that?" Simon asked, knowing the answer already.

Nick stood, adjusted his Armani suit, picked a piece of non-existent lint from his shoulder before answering the question. "Let's see…you had additional security cameras added to your place that now cover the entrance and rear of her salon. You get here early in the morning and stay late at night so you can be here when she arrives and when she leaves."

"I do no such thing. I was home yesterday before the evening news," Simon countered.

Nick ignored him and continued, "You hired parking security for when you are not here in the evenings. Brother, you are obvious to anyone paying attention. Now, take a lesson from someone who knows what he's talking about. Go make your interest known."

Taking a glance at his cell phone, Nick walked toward the front door of the barbershop, "Simon, do it today," he laughed and left through the door.

Was he really that transparent? Simon thought about his attraction to Karleigh. It was strange, kind of coming out of nowhere. One day he was all business-minded, and the next day he was protective of a woman who won't go to breakfast with him. His feelings for Karleigh were difficult for him to quantify.

Simon had a rather unexciting social life growing up as a teenager. Girls flirted with him, yet he hadn't entirely accepted his good looks. Computers were more his object of affection. As an adult, women were known to fawn over him, but he rarely gave them any notice. The woman he was genuinely attracted to caused his palms to sweat, and his pulse to increase every time he was in her presence. Simon wasn't even nervous in the board room or around the rich and famous, but with Karleigh, his nerves felt like lead in his veins.

Just thinking about asking her on a date again had his mouth dry and in need of water. He wasn't going to let her win by continuing to turn him down. He was going to gather some strength and keep asking until he wore down her resistance, or he ran home crying. Whichever came first.

*****

Karleigh was alone in her office, tallying up the end of day sales receipts. She wasn't where she wanted to be financially for the completion of her first month, but she wasn't behind, either. Even after all the drama with the grand opening and spending money for a new window, she held her head high, stuck to her guns and continued with the plan.

The salon now had a new security system with video monitoring and intercom. She could see her parking lot and the front and rear entrances. The security team that Simon referred gave her an excellent deal on her monitoring service. She initially assumed that Simon had something to do with the crazy steep discount. It was a deal that was too good to be true.

After checking with other security companies, she found none of them could come close to the deal she was getting. The Security Guys assured her that Simon Sharpe had nothing to do with the quote they offered, but when the guy told her this, Karleigh thought she saw a flicker of humor behind his eyes.

Nevertheless, Karleigh couldn't afford what the other companies were quoting, so she stayed with The Security Guys. They proved to be top-notch regarding customer service. For that reason alone, she would forgive Simon Sharpe if he did have something to do with it.

Someone rang the doorbell, and the notification buzzed Karleigh's cell phone. She wasn't closed for the evening, but she kept her doors locked when she was alone. The person at the door was standing with their back to the camera. Karleigh could tell it was a woman by the skinny jeans she was wearing and the huge handbag she carried over her right forearm.

Instead of asking for the person's name, Karleigh absently buzzed the woman in. She stepped out of her office into the salon and found Alicia standing in the middle of her lobby.

Alicia Whitsett was a stylist that Karleigh previously worked with at the Mane Event. They never got along, and Karleigh made it a point to stay far away from each other as much as possible. Alicia had been at the Mane Event for a year before Karleigh arrived. Her attitude toward the new girl did not go unnoticed. Karleigh wondered why Alicia hated her, but she was quickly informed by other stylists that Alicia hated everyone.

"Well, I guess your little opening day issue didn't deter you," Alicia said, laced with venom. "How's business?" She strutted over toward the glass cases that had Karleigh's hair care products displayed. She took a single finger and wiped across the shelf, trying to find dust.

Karleigh didn't understand why Alicia continued to harass her. She was a pain in the rear when she worked at the Mane Event, and now that Karleigh was gone, she should be happy.

Alicia believed herself to be the best stylist in all of the city. Her over-inflated self-worth was brought on because a reality star gave her a shout out on their television show. Ever since her clientele increased ten-fold, and she started doing hair tutorials on the internet.

Alicia was good at trendy hairstyles, but she didn't care about the health of the hair. Karleigh focused on healthy hair care and education for her clients. Some stylists thought she was losing business by only focusing on healthy hair instead of trends, but Karleigh knew her clients would return when they saw the results they wanted.

Women who wanted their hair dipped, dyed and fried, just to look like Beyoncé or Kim K. would pay significant bucks for Alicia to turn them into a knockoff version of a celebrity. In a few months, those same ladies would need deep conditioning treatments or even haircuts to get rid of the damaged hair.

That was what made Karleigh so different. She focused on the health of hair and not just a trendy style. Karleigh was known to turn clients away if they were adamant about damaging their hair.

"Not that it is any of your concern, but business is good." Karleigh walked over to an empty station and started reorganizing items to appear busy. "What can I help you with?"

"I just wanted to see your *little* salon. All cleaned up, that is. The last time I was here, you didn't have a front window. Did daddy pay for that, too?"

Karleigh didn't miss the dig that her father had something to do with financing her salon. Her parents did give her a loan, but most of the financing was her savings. Also, she didn't remember Alicia being at the grand opening. There had been so many people milling around and so much activity happening, it would have been easy for Karleigh to miss her.

She had enough of Alicia and her innuendos and disrespect. Karleigh charged to the front door and held it open. "Alicia, say what you want, think what you want, but you are not welcome here. You can leave."

Alicia sauntered around slowly, making sure to drag out the scene she was causing. Karleigh stood, unmoved, and waited with the door opened.

"It's so small in here, how many clients can you serve, one at a time?" she took her time walking toward the entrance.

The Mane Event hair salon was very spacious and had booth space for 16 stylists. But the stations were so close to one another stylists often bumped into each other. The salon also had limited storage space for a stylist's product. At Serenity, there were six stations with plenty of storage space, and Karleigh was proud of that.

Karleigh refused to answer Alicia, instead, just continuing to hold the door open.

"I guess I will see you around. Don't plan to enter the hair show next month. You will only embarrass yourself."

Karleigh shut and locked the door behind Alicia, barely letting her clear the doorway. She had completely forgotten about the hair show. The Annual Hair and Beauty Convention was the premiere event in town for professionals in the beauty industry. The convention lasted for 4 days and was a place for beauty professionals to get together for product education, meet with vendors, learn new techniques, and more. She had forgotten she paid her registration fee a few months ago.

The convention always ended with a hair show to showcase the latest hairstyles and make-up trends. It was considered the academy awards for hairstylists. Usually, Karleigh wouldn't enter any of the competitions. She wasn't competitive and only attended the events for the education being provided and to find new products.

Other stylists lived for the hair show. Especially the stylists at The Mane Event. Ms. Carter encouraged her girls to register. And, by encouraging, she borderline forced them to participate. Except for Karleigh, she never pushed her one way or the other. The truth was, Karleigh's styles were the reason women came to the Mane Event.

Ms. Carter recognized that Karleigh kept a steady stream of clientele, and they raved all over town about their hair. Her clients may have been older, but they loved their hair and rarely shied away from letting other women know.

A knocking on the front door brought Karleigh out from her thoughts. When she saw Simon standing there, she was relieved that it wasn't Alicia again. She opened the door but blocked his entrance. Karleigh was not interested in having a long conversation with Simon. She was tired and ready to go home. "Hey, Simon. What's up?"

"I noticed you were still here for the evening. Working late? I saw your client just leave."

"She was not my client," Karleigh quickly corrected him.

"Oh, well, I saw her leave. I was wondering if you would like to grab a cup of coffee?"

Simon seemed uneasy around her, Karleigh had never noticed how he would shove his hands into his pockets until now. She wondered if he was afraid to ask her out again? But why would that be the case? Did he think that she would snap on him? Well, their last few interactions hadn't been warm or welcoming, but they were cordial. She had no real reason not to accept his offer. Her day had been long, and she was ready to go home. But this time, instead of saying no, she asked, "Coffee? Where?"

"I was thinking about going to the Java House down the street. Not too far. We could even walk, it's a nice night," he nervously shifted from one foot to the other.

She pondered this for a few seconds. There were a few things she wanted to talk to Simon about, mainly the security discount and maybe even the hair show. He had been in business much longer than she had, and he may be able to offer some business tips and suggestions.

"Alright, let me grab my jacket." She was about to close the door in his face when he stepped inside.

"So, you were going to just leave me out there," he said with a laugh. "I'm harmless, I promise. He put his hands up in front of him.

"Sorry about that," Karleigh sheepishly walked away. She didn't know why she always remained cautious, and often rude around Simon. Before the end of the night, she would have to apologize to him for her attitude and hope he could relate to the stress she was under. His offer of coffee came at a perfect time, though. Karleigh needed a break away from the salon and needed to forget about Alicia coming into her space.

She grabbed her jacket and purse, locked her office door, turned off the lights in the back, and set the alarm. They had 15 seconds to leave out the front door. Simon must have known that because he held the door opened and waited for her to exit.

The night was nice, like Simon mentioned. A soft breeze blowing against her face calmed her agitated nerves. While they walked across the parking lot in silence, she wondered what he was thinking. The new girl on the block starting all this trouble. His business was probably being affected by her taking up space and causing problems.

She had so many questions to ask him but momentarily refrained, enjoying the silence. When they came to the first corner, they began to talk at the same time.

"Ladies first," Simon offered.

"I'm sorry about how I've been acting lately. It's the stress of being a business owner. I have questions for you. Do you mind if I pick your brain about a few things, business-related?" Karleigh quickly clarified her intent.

"Absolutely. You can ask me anything," he replied.

She noticed he was doing it again. That unsure body language, like he was afraid Karleigh would go off on him or maybe he was scared of rejection. She had read in a women's magazine how the most attractive men often struggled with rejection. His behavior puzzled her.

Their walk to the Java house was the first time Karleigh really paid attention to her neighborhood. She had been so focused on finding the right location for her salon, and then, preparing to be successful, she had not gotten a full look at her surroundings.

There were several small shops and offices on both sides of the street. The Java House was only three blocks from the salon. Next door to the Java House was a store that specialized in all things made of silver, and on the other side was a consignment clothing boutique. The neighborhood was unique and eclectic.

The Java House was a small, intimate coffee house with very minimal furnishings. The coffee aroma was warm and inviting from the moment you opened the door. Simon was able to find a small table in the back. Karleigh noticed the tables were made of natural dark wood, and the chairs were all mismatched, made of metal, wood, or plastic. There was also soft music playing in the background that didn't overpower the groups of people talking among one another.

"This is a nice place. Do you come here often?" Karleigh asked.

Simon smiled before answering her. "That's a great pick-up line, you know. I come here enough."

They stepped up to the counter, and the barista called him by name. *Guess he does come here often*, Karleigh thought. He had been in the neighborhood for a while, so it made sense that many people around would know him.

Once they ordered their coffees and were seated at their table, Karleigh continued with her questions. "So, what do you think about the hair show? Have you ever participated?" she asked.

"The last time I attended the hair show was about eight years ago. I was still trying to build my business. Since then, my clientele has picked up, and I'm comfortable with the products I use. Besides, It's mostly for women anyways."

Karleigh tried to give him a stern and severe look but failed miserably when she started laughing. "I was about to get mad with you for saying that, but I realized you are right. The hair show is a place for female stylists to show off in front of other stylists. They have a little section in the back for barbers."

They had a relaxed conversation and fun banter back and forth about the beauty industry and being new to owning her own business. Simon told her stories about his first year in business and the ups and downs he endured in his first location. Karleigh hadn't laughed this much in months. It had been a long time since she had been in the company of a man who was not related to her. Simon wasn't pretentious like she first thought, he was just very down to earth.

"Enough business talk for a minute. Let's talk about something else," she wanted to change the subject.

"Okay, tell me about growing up with sisters. What was that like? Four teenage girls in the house at once." Simon asked between sips of coffee.

"Well, you know I'm the oldest. There are two years between Me, Poe, and Karmyn. Kyna is the baby and is 10 years younger than me. Mom was trying to give dad a boy, but it wasn't in God's plans." She took a sip of her coffee, trying to decide what information to divulge with Simon. "We didn't spend much time with Kyna, that's why she is so spoiled. Even though I'm the oldest, Karmyn acted the oldest, and Poe was just being Poe. By the time I graduated from high school, Poe was a sophomore, and Karmyn had accelerated a grade, so she was a freshman. Poor Kyna was still in elementary school."

Karleigh didn't want to talk about herself anymore. Instead, she wanted to know more about Simon. "Tell me more about you?"

"What do you want to know?"

"About your childhood, your sister, anything you want me to know."

Simon's jaw clenched, he averted his eyes to stare at the floor. Karleigh wanted to take the question back because of the pained expression he tried to hide. He looked like he was trying to suppress some horrific memory. She was going to apologize for asking the question, but then he relaxed and slapped on his killer smile before saying, "I had a sister, Sylvia. She was younger than me. Growing up was easy for us. My parents had one rule, do good in school, and get whatever you want."

She was going to ask another question, but he quickly changed the subject. "Did you find a security company?"

Karleigh decided to let the subject of his sister go. Whatever it was he was hiding, was none of her business. She shouldn't get that personal with him anyways. They weren't in a relationship, she didn't need to know. However, she did have questions about the security company. "Simon, be honest, did you tell the Security Guys to give me a discount?"

"Honestly, I did not," he answered with a straight face.

"Then, what did you do?" she asked, short of accusing him of anything. "They gave me a super deal and discount compared to other companies."

"You have to promise not to get angry."

Too late, her attitude had surfaced. When people start off their sentences with disclaimer statements, they are always going to say something that will cause the reason for the disclaimer. So, telling her not to get angry caused her to become inflamed, and she didn't even know why yet.

"I will make no such promise."

Simon laughed. "Well, then I'm not saying anything. We were having a good, friendly time. I'm not going to ruin it now."

Karleigh was even more visibly upset now. She stood and waited a full three seconds, then proceeded out the door. Simon didn't immediately follow her, and she was grateful for that. She was tired of people, men, explicitly withholding information from her. But, like the other times, she was probably jumping to conclusions. She had to work on that knee-jerk reaction.

Simon eventually caught up to her at the end of the first block. He didn't say anything while they continued to walk back to the salon. The familiar feeling of dread washed over her again. Karleigh's heart started beating faster and faster, the closer she got to her salon. She was almost in tears when she saw her building was still intact. But, the feeling was still present.

She didn't know why until she turned to tell Simon good night. That's when she saw her car. It was initially blocked from view by someone's SUV. Simon must have seen her face because he turned around to see it, too. Someone had spray-painted "Loser" all over her car.

"No! No! No!" Karleigh yelled as she ran toward, yet, another piece of her property destroyed. "Why is someone doing this to me?" When she didn't get an answer from Simon, she turned to him. He was already on the phone with the police.

Karleigh was convinced now, more than ever, that being a business owner might not be in God's plan for her. But then another of Poe's common sayings came to mind, *"He didn't bring you this far to leave you."* Closing her eyes, Karleigh started silently praying. These days it seemed prayer was an all-day occurrence.

Chapter 12

Karleigh felt like this was déjà vu. The scene was all too familiar. Police were arriving again, along with Nick and Karmyn. With those two around each other, it was bound to be drama. Hopefully, they would remain respectful to one another, at least while the police were there. That may have been too much to ask. Karmyn pulled up in her Range Rover and parked in front of Nick, blocking his access to the parking spot he was about to take.

Karmyn jumped from her car and raced toward her. "Karleigh, are you okay?" her sister asked, full of concern.

"Why does this keep happening to me? Do you think it's a sign? That maybe I'm not supposed to be in business." Before her sister could answer, Karleigh continued talking. "Maybe God is trying to tell me to cut my losses." Utterly defeated, Karleigh walked away from Karmyn, Nick and Simon.

"Hey!" Simon grabbed her shoulders and turned her around. "You don't honestly believe that, do you?"

Nick was about to speak, but Karmyn interrupted him, "Sister, your faith is stronger than mine. This…," she said, motioning toward the car, "…is not God's work. You have to trust that everything will work out."

"We will find out who is doing this to you," Nick added.

Karleigh took a deep breath and tried to summon all of her faith. Doing so was proving to be challenging. She was willing to accept that, maybe, there was something for her to learn from all of this. But, she didn't understand why it had to hurt so bad.

After the police questioned everyone, they headed back into the salon to sit down for a breather. Karleigh was still unsure of everything. Especially Simon. He had already called the security monitoring place before she even thought about it. He had her car towed to his automotive body shop and had her file a claim with her insurance company. He was taking care of her like she was his girlfriend or wife.

Wife? That thought had Karleigh thinking about his motivation, again. What did he want from her? In her experience, men just didn't do this kind of thing for women they were not in a relationship with unless there was an ulterior motive. Karleigh needed to know what that motive was.

She didn't know how to feel about him taking charge like he did. But, on the other hand, she needed him to do those things because she had not been thinking straight. Even once Karmyn showed up, she was still wallowing in self-pity. Karleigh was having a difficult time understanding why God allowed these things to happen to her when she did everything right.

"You know what guys? I'm exhausted. I just want to go home." She looked to her sister, "Karmyn, can you drop me off at home.?"

"Actually, I was on my way to the gym. I can take you afterward. I'll only be about 30-45 minutes."

"Ugh....fine," Karleigh said, exasperatedly.

"I can take you home," Simon volunteered.

"Thanks, Simon, but Karmyn…"

"Is very busy and would appreciate it if you could take her home," Karmyn jumped in.

The two sisters had an intense stare down before Karmyn broke eye contact.

"Well, that's settled. See you later, sister." Karmyn grabbed her keys, gave her sister a kiss on the cheek, and left.

The nerve of her sister, pawning her off on Simon. The next time she saw her, she would figure out a way to get her back. In the back of Karleigh's mind, she heard God's voice say, *"Vengeance is mine."* And now getting even was a disappearing thought.

Nick followed behind Karmyn, leaving Karleigh with a promise that they would find out who was behind this. He kissed her cheek, gave Simon a slap on the back, and left.

With Karmyn and Nick gone, her thoughts were back to Simon. Why would he be so eager to drive her home? Before she saw the damage to her car, she had been mad at him, and now she was appreciative that he was there. Drastically switching emotions around him were becoming too frequent and draining.

"Before you get any ideas, I know you're still mad at me. To answer your question from the coffee shop, yes, I talked to the Security Guys. You have the discount you have because I added you to my account. I don't have access to your cameras or anything like that, but by adding you, it got you a bigger discount."

"Why would you do that?" Karleigh asked. "Why are you doing any of this?"

Karleigh watched Simon slowly walk toward her. He was self-assured and confident, where she was afraid of taking risks. He enclosed both of her hands in his and said, "I remember what it's like to be a new business owner. Starting out with limited funds. I just want to help you."

She considered his response before speaking. "I don't know many men like you. Men that just help without wanting something in return."

"Well, I wish there were more men like me. All men aren't out to get something. Some of us, good men, just want to help."

*****

Simon watched Karleigh as she glared at him. He just hoped she wouldn't stay mad for very long. When she did speak, he thought she was about to blow up. Instead, she said, 'thank you." Simon felt like he dodged a bullet with that one.

They locked up the place for the second time that night and walked to his car. He made sure to open her door, assist her inside of the vehicle, and wait for her to put on her seat belt before driving away. She stayed quiet for the ride to her house. Simon took a few glances in her direction as she told him where to turn, but she mostly kept her eyes closed.

Simon worried about her. She seemed to have given up on her dream with just a minor setback. He remembered after the first attack, Karleigh bounced right back, and would not let that break-in deter her. More determined than ever, she made do with what she had to have a great event. Why was this time any different?

The neighborhood where Karleigh lived wasn't very far from the salon. He pulled his car into her driveway and waited for her to make the next move. Would she talk to him or get out of the car? They remained in the vehicle, occupied by their own thoughts, listening to the sounds of the smooth jazz radio station. Simon didn't take her for a smooth jazz kind of lady, but she kept her eyes closed and seemed to relax.

He couldn't seem to understand why anyone would want to sabotage Karleigh. Other than her temper, and her always jumping to the wrong conclusions with limited information, she was a caring, hardworking woman. Simon's thoughts jumped from it being random attacks to a jealous boyfriend or the girlfriend of a guy she had been dating. Karleigh didn't seem like the type to become involved in drama like that, so he quickly erased that option. Typically, men wouldn't resort to property vandalism at the loss of a relationship. He scratched that one off the list.

Since neither seemed inclined to get out of the car, Simon asked, "How long have you lived in this neighborhood?"

Devoid of all emotion, she responded, "About five years. I knew the previous owners. They retired and moved to Florida. They practically gave me the house."

The neighborhood looked older and well-established. The streets were lined with large oak and maple trees. All the homes appeared worn but loved. This was the type of neighborhood people raised their families in. Homes in this area rarely went for sale because families stayed long term. Children would move into their parents' home when the time came, keeping the house in the family.

When Simon looked in her direction, she was staring straight ahead. Even though she answered the question, she didn't seem to be present.

"Earth to Karleigh. Where are you right now?" he asked.

"What do you mean? I'm right here," she responded, clearly annoyed by the question.

"I mean, where is your head right now? What are you thinking about?"

"I'm thinking about if I am truly following God's plan, or did I make this up in my own head."

Simon didn't have an answer for her. There were days when he questioned his business decisions himself. What he did know was Karleigh was a woman of faith. Having faith meant believing God would handle things, even if you couldn't see how.

"Remember what Karmyn told you. Don't put a period where God put a comma. This is just a comma moment. This is your dream, your passion, and your purpose."

"Do you go to church Simon?" she asked.

Chapter 13

Karleigh stunned herself when she asked Simon that question. She wasn't the type to randomly ask people about their religious beliefs. But, if she even thought that their friendship might turn into more, she needed to know that he believed in God.

"I do. My family has been going to Eden Missionary Baptist Church for over 20 years. What church do you attend?"

"My family has been members at Mount Olive for over 70 years. My grandmother was baptized there, and all her siblings and all of their children. I think my great-grandmother was a founding member." She smiled for the first time since finding her car vandalized. Thinking of her great-grandmother always made her smile.

Karleigh knew she needed to get out of his car; she fumbled with her keys for a few seconds. She was exhibiting nervous behavior; but, why would she be worried? Simon, being the ultimate gentleman, exited the vehicle first to walk around the car and open her door. She waited for Simon to open her car door and walk her to the front door. "I appreciate you taking care of everything this evening. I know I totally spaced out."

"Hey, don't worry about it," Simon said. They both stood on her front porch in awkward silence. Neither knew how to end the evening.

Simon blurted out, "What are your plans for tomorrow?"

"I have to go to church in the morning. Then, my parents still have family dinner afterward. It's sort of required until we have families of our own." She adjusted her purse on her shoulder then asked, "Would you like to go to church with me?"

"Church? With you and your family?"

"You don't have to…" Karleigh turned her back to him so that he couldn't see the embarrassment on her face.

"What time should I pick you up?"

"Pick me up? I don't understand. You can just meet me at the church."

Simon gently grabbed her hand, "Karleigh, how do you usually get to church?"

"I drive," she started to say, but quickly realized her situation. "But I don't have a car."

"Exactly. How about, I pick you up for church, and then, after service, I can take you to get a rental car."

"I don't know if I can afford a rental car. I may just take the bus in the mornings and have one of my sisters bring me home in the evenings."

"I have a better idea. How about I loan you one of my cars. Before you say no, I have several vehicles, and I don't mind you driving one until you get yours back."

She had never met a man like Simon. He was thoughtful and caring and didn't want anything in return. "Are you sure about that?" She asked.

"Absolutely. What time should I pick you up?"

Karleigh was hesitant, giving him her now-infamous stare down while in thought. "10:00 A.M., and don't be late. My grandmother hates when any of us are late for praise and worship."

"Go inside, lock the door, and I will see you in the morning." He smiled, kissed the back of her hand, and waited for her to follow instructions.

Karleigh locked the door as she was told. With her back to the door, she slowly descended to the floor. She couldn't believe what was happening. Simon was like a real-life knight in shining armor. He always arrived just in time to save the day.

She wasn't sure if that was a good thing or a bad thing. If she had too many damsel in distress moments, he might think she wasn't worth the effort. But, she didn't want to be worth the effort. Building her business should be her priority, not always thinking about the attractive barber that worked next door. Men and relationships were not supposed to be her focus. But, whenever Simon was around, she seemed to lose all concentration.

Karleigh gathered herself from the floor and went to her kitchen in search of a late-night snack. Whenever she was nervous about something, she turned to food. If it weren't for her sister being a personal fitness trainer, Karleigh would probably be overweight from the late nights and stress eating she would do.

The rumble in her stomach was a reminder she hadn't eaten anything since breakfast. Karleigh had not gotten around to grocery shopping in weeks, instead opting for take-out during her busy days. Finding nothing she really wanted to eat in her refrigerator, she had to settle for a ham and cheese sandwich. The first bite of her sandwich was heavenly.

She finished her lunch and was cleaning the kitchen when her phone rang from the other room. Karleigh tried to guess what sister this could be. Probably Kyna at this time of night. Shockingly, it was Poe calling.

"Sister, I just found out about your car. What are you going to do?"

"I had it sent to the repair shop. Simon offered to let me drive one of his cars until mine is back."

"He did, now? Well, that was extremely kind of him."

"Seriously, Poe, he is just a kind and caring man."

"Kind is taking you home. Kind is offering to pick you up for work. Men don't just loan their cars to women. Some men treat their cars better than their spouses," Poe paused, letting that last statement sink in with Karleigh. "So, you still think he doesn't have a thing for you?"

"Yeah, well…I kind of have a thing for him now." Karleigh heard some clicking noises. "Poe, are you there? Can you hear me?"

"Oh, I can hear you, and so can Kyna and Karmyn."

Her sister was unbelievable. In a matter of seconds, she had conferenced her other sisters into the call. Karleigh wanted to share this new revelation with one sister, not all of them. "Why did you call them?"

"Because I needed witnesses to this minor miracle. Go ahead, sister. Repeat what you just told me," Poe laughed.

"Fine, I think I have a thing for Simon Sharpe. There, are you happy?" Karleigh had walked to her bedroom and plopped down on her bed. She was actually okay with her sisters knowing. They were her best friends, and she did need someone to discuss these crazy emotions with.

There was silence on the phone, and then all three sisters started laughing. "Tell us something we didn't know," Karmyn said.

"I've only been around you two once, and I could see the sparks flying. You conferenced us for this. Goodnight, sisters," Kyna laughed as she disconnected the phone.

"Well, I guess Kyna will find out tomorrow that I invited Simon to church in the morning."

Karmyn and Poe, clearly shocked, screamed through the phone, "You did what?"

*****

Simon activated the Bluetooth system in his car and called the one person who could tell him if he was crazy or not. "Nick, we gotta talk."

"Right now? I'm in the middle of something."

"Yes! Right now. Meet me at the shop."

Simon ended the call and headed back to the barbershop. When he pulled up, Nick was waiting at the door.

"How did you get here so fast?"

"I was at the Java house. What's so important?"

Simon turned off the alarm when they entered. Instead of sitting in the barber chairs like they usually would, they went back to his office. Simon told Nick about everything that had happened after he left them alone in the salon. Then, he dropped the bomb on Nick.

"She invited me to church with her in the morning. And I accepted the invitation."

"Whoa, that's a big step? Going to church with her and her family is like...is like...the last step before marriage."

Scrubbing his hands down his face, Simon agreed. "Yeah, I know. The really crazy thing about it is I *want* to go to church with her."

Nick had been standing near the door. "Maybe I should sit down," he said, as he took the seat closest to Simon's desk and leaned back. "When was the last time you've been to church? Not just inside of one, but to an actual Sunday service?"

Simon had to think about that question. He believed in God, he just didn't believe you needed to go to church every week. He read his bible, sporadically, but he did read it. Now that he had time to think about it, Simon recalled the last time he was in church was the worst day of his life.

She survived 12 days after her accident. His sister Sylvia was 22 years old when she took her life and the life of her ex-boyfriend. She had found evidence that the young man was cheating on her. She tried to confront him while they were driving home from a movie.

Sylvia had suspected he was cheating for a long time but never approached the situation until she had proof. She gave him several opportunities to come clean, but he never did. So, when she found the evidence, she couldn't take his lies anymore and drove them both into a nearby lake.

Simon prayed for them both to survive. He wanted the young man to feel the pain he was feeling at the time. Instead, they both died a few hours apart. Sylvia's funeral was the last time he was in a church. And now he willingly accepted an invitation to go back.

He shook off the memory and told Nick, "Well, I'm going to church tomorrow."

"Does Karleigh know how you feel about her?"

"What do you mean? I barely know how I feel. A few months ago, she barged into my space with her salon. Messed up all the plans I was working on. And now, here I am, taking care of her car, paying for her security system."

Nick threw his hands in the air. "Back up. You're paying for her security system? That's news to me."

"Yeah, well, she's a new business owner with limited funds."

"So, what? She should have to struggle just like the rest of us." Nick shook his head back and forth. "Dude, you got it bad. Let me get out of here before whatever it is you have, rubs off on me." Nick walked out of the office. Simon heard the front door open and close leaving him alone with his thoughts and feelings about Karleigh Hammond.

She was a pain in his side, jumping from one emotion to the next, Karleigh was what he envisioned his wife to be like. He sat in his office, trying to figure out why these emotions were so sudden. Before he met Karleigh, he had not been interested in any woman. He hadn't even had thoughts of marriage. But, now, it's all he could think of.

Chapter 14

As promised, Simon arrived at Karleigh's house on time, and she was ready and waiting. She earned another point in his book for not making him wait. She was dressed in a long-sleeve, navy blue dress that stopped just beneath the knee. On any other woman, this dress would make them look like an old lady. But Karleigh made the dress alluring. She paired it with a pair of gold high heels and a pair of simple gold hoop earrings.

Simon was noticing things about her that he never saw on other women. He never cared about a woman's jewelry or clothing accessories before. Now, his observations were puzzling. He was still grappling with his feelings for her.

After exchanging morning pleasantries, he escorted Karleigh to the car and opened the door for her. Exhaling a deep breath, he slowly walked to the driver's side. Being in church with her may prove to be a more significant challenge than he thought.

They drove to church in near silence, only soft sounds from the radio played in the background. Simon was grateful for the quiet because he needed to concentrate on not saying or doing anything stupid, especially in front of her family. He had to keep his cool when everything about Karleigh had his insides going chaotic.

Eden Missionary Baptist Church was in the middle of a quiet neighborhood near Simon's old high school. The church must have had a large membership because they had to park two blocks away. On the walk to the church, Simon reached out to hold Karleigh's hand, and to his surprise, she didn't pull away from him.

The praise team was rocking from the minute they entered the sanctuary. Simon liked the country style interior of the church. Exposed beams and stained glass windows reminded him of the small churches in the south he would visit during family reunions.

The comfortable feeling put him at ease. Or it could have been the way Karleigh was rubbing her thumb across his hand. When he looked at her, she gave him a reassuring smile. Could she sense he hadn't been in church in a long while?

Her sisters saved them a seat in the middle of the church. He was grateful they didn't have to sit all the way upfront with her parents and grandmother. Church service was a total of 90 minutes, and it didn't feel like they had been there all day. The pastor had preached about restoring the faith when things don't go your way. Simon thought that sermon was made for Karleigh.

After service, they met her parents at the front of the church sanctuary.

"Well, hello, Simon. It's nice to see you again," Kyra greeted him.

"Nice seeing you again, Mrs. Hammond," Simon replied.

"You can call me, Ms. Kyra. Mrs. Hammond is Karleigh's grandmother." Kyra motioned to a vibrant octogenarian. Erma Hammond was 81 years young, and she didn't use the aid of any devices to help her get around. She was silver-haired and wore it in loose curls, which hung below her shoulders.

"There is no way this young woman is a grandmother. How do you do, Mrs. Hammond?" Simon sweetly asked, taking her hand in his.

"Karleigh, this one here is smooth as a penny, but I like him. You keep him around. Good for my self-esteem." Grandma Hammond smiled at Simon.

Karleigh rolled her eyes and laughed, "Grandma, there is nothing wrong with your self-esteem."

Simon chatted with the Hammonds for another ten minutes before the ushers gently began escorting people out of the sanctuary. He found himself genuinely enjoying being in church again. There was a time when the church held good memories for him versus the ones he previously dealt with after his sister's death.

Karleigh hadn't attempted any more outward displays of affection after they had entered the church. She was throwing off inconsistent vibes, and that was making Simon go crazy with questions. She held his hand when they entered the church, but afterward did everything she could to keep her hands to herself.

"Simon, we have family dinner after church every week, would you like to join us?" Kyra asked.

"Oh, no, Mom. Simon was just kind enough to bring me to church. I can ride with one of you back to the house."

"Karleigh, we still need to get you a car. Did you forget I am loaning you one of mine?" He smiled sweetly, then turned to Kyra. "Ms. Kyra, I would love to join your family for dinner."

"We eat dinner at three, would you be able to get the car afterward?" her mother asked.

Karleigh gave him a look that said, *"we will talk about this later,"* then, her smile returned. Simon knew he was going to hear a mouthful later, and he was ready for her. The talk had to wait because Karleigh's grandmother insisted she ride to the house with Karleigh and Simon.

The 15-minute ride was chocked full of family information that Simon was sure Karleigh didn't want him to know. Mrs. Hammond gushed over her granddaughters and especially praised Karleigh and her accomplishments.

The elder Hammonds had a large home in a new housing development just outside of the city limits. Karleigh's father invited him into the refuge of the man cave in his basement. The basement was decked out in paraphernalia from every type of sport imaginable. Simon immediately walked over to the life-size cut-out of Joe Louis.

"The Brown Bomber," Simon whispered.

"What do you know about Joe Louis?" Kevin spoke.

"Greatest boxer of his time," Simon replied.

Simon felt Karleigh's father sizing him up. This was to be expected. Her father told him none of his girls invited young men over for dinner or for any other reason. Simon tucked that piece of information away with the others.

Kevin Hammond briefly mentioned Karmyn's ex-husband, but Simon could tell the family didn't care for the man much. The two men talked about all things sports and more until they were called upstairs for dinner.

Mr. Hammond sat at the head of the table. He grabbed his wife's hand, who sat to his right, and then she grabbed Karleigh's hand, who sat next to her. They went around the table until Kyna, who sat to her father's left side, held his hand. Kevin, then, said grace before everyone reached for their plates in a free-for-all.

As expected, dinner was fantastic. "Ms. Kyra, dinner was delicious. I haven't had a home-cooked meal like that in years."

"Really? You don't eat with your family?" Karleigh asked.

"My family usually caters for big events. My mom is a vegan but never pushed us to follow her. So, she tends to only cook vegan dishes. A man can only eat so much tofu," Simon laughed.

"Oh. Well, Kyna would love your mother. She, too, only eats leaves," Kyra said.

"Mother, I eat more than leaves," Kyna replied.

Karleigh answered for Kyna. "She's not vegan, but she likes vegan dishes."

"Exactly, I still eat butter and cheese."

The family had an easy conversation, but no one talked about Karleigh or her salon. It made Simon wonder if anyone other than Karmyn knew what had happened.

They didn't stay long after dinner was finished. Simon drove to his house so Karleigh could borrow one of his vehicles. At least that was the primary reason. He also wanted to get her off of her turf and onto his.

*****

Shocked didn't adequately describe how Karleigh felt when she saw his home. He lived in a secluded, gated community not far from her house.

There were about 4 or 5 other homes through the gate. Each sitting on at least 10-acres of land.

Karleigh used to dream of having a house like his. One with a wrap-around country style porch, and two white wicker rocking chairs, just like Simon had. He even had rose bushes planted around one side of the house.

Upon first sight, the house reminded her of a Country Living magazine cover she had seen. She could imagine sitting on the porch, drinking her lemonade or sweet tea, and watching her children play in the enormous yard. Karleigh had no idea where the thought of children came from, and she quickly erased it from her mind.

"From the way your jaw dropped, I take it you like it," Simon asked.

"I love it. Do you live here alone?"

"Sunday through Wednesday. Thursday, Friday, and Saturday, I stay at my condo in the city. My more upscale clients like to have fresh cuts before going out on the town, so I need to be readily available."

"I feel like I've seen your house before. It's beautiful, country–chic."

"If you read housing or decorator magazines, then you probably have. This house has been in over 30 magazines across the world. Come in, let me show you around."

Karleigh felt like her jaw would never close. The inside was the opposite of the country outside. Every room inside was ultra-modern. The kitchen was a chef's paradise, duel stovetops, extra deep sink, and a beautiful island in the middle, large enough to seat six people on one side.

The back yard was not at all what Karleigh was expecting. The sunroom led out onto a beautiful deck that overlooked a large patio and swimming pool. The pool had a slide on one end and a waterfall on the other side. Off into the distance, Karleigh thought she heard horses.

"Who has horses?"

"I do." He pointed to their left, leading to a stable in the distance. "I have two retired racing horses. I breed them."

Karleigh was utterly overwhelmed. She had not imagined that Simon Sharpe, barber to the rich and famous, would enjoy country living at its finest. She was seeing a side of him she never envisioned.

"Let me take you over to the garage. I have a few cars I like to drive when the mood hits me." He grabbed her hand and pulled her in the opposite direction.

The garage housed four vehicles and had a bay area just like in a mechanic car shop.

Karleigh was captivated by all she was seeing. "Do you work on your cars in here?"

"It's a hobby of mine. I can relax and unwind when I'm restoring old cars. I sold the last one I worked on. A 1971 ruby red Corvette."

"Okay, so which car can I drive?" Karleigh tried to keep her excitement down, but she felt like a kid in the toy store.

"Any of the vehicles in here or outside."

Behind the garage was a huge SUV, an Infiniti sedan, a Toyota, and a Mini Cooper. "I never took you for the type to drive a Mini Cooper," she laughed.

"Well, after watching one of my favorite movies, The Italian Job, I had to have one."

"And I guess silver is your favorite color." Most of the vehicles, except the Mini Cooper, were silver. The Mini was orange.

"Actually, my favorite color is blue. The silver thing was unintentional. The orange that is all my god-daughter. She talked me into it.

Karleigh looked around and figured the SUV was much too big and the mini cooper too small. That left the Infiniti and the Toyota. Since she had never driven an Infiniti, she walked toward it. She immediately noticed the leather seats and the gadgets on the dashboard.

"I guess it's the Infiniti for you," Simon entered a code to open the doors and allowed Karleigh to sit in the driver's seat.

"Are you sure you don't mind? It should only be for a couple of days, right?"

Simon's cell phone began ringing, interrupting their conversation. He held up a finger, indicating he would need a minute. That was fine, because she needed a minute, as well. She was still trying to accept his kindness and everything he had done so far.

"Sorry about that. I have to take care of some things," Simon said. "You are welcomed to stay, walk around the property, or check out the house. Just don't leave. I will only need a few minutes."

"Okay. It's no problem." Karleigh was still intrigued by Simon. He was single but had a beautiful farmhouse on acres of land. She wanted to know more about the man and thought that walking around his house would tell her more.

*****

Simon walked back into the house and into his office, "What's going on, Nick?"

"Well, the vandal wasn't too smart. I checked the cars in the parking lot from the night Karleigh's salon got destroyed and compared them against the vehicles from last night. Only one showed up both times."

Simon was afraid the attack was personal. He didn't want to believe someone was deliberately targeting Karleigh or her salon, but the evidence was unraveling in that direction. He had been in that neighborhood for years, and nothing like this had happened to any of the other businesses.

Nick continued, "Well, you are not going to believe who the car belongs to."

"Come on, Nick, don't keep me guessing." Simon was getting frustrated.

"A woman by the name of Alicia Whitsett. She seems to be another hairstylist. Guess what salon?"

"Come on, man, stop with the suspense and games."

"She currently works at The Mane Event."

"That's where Karleigh used to work." Simon was peering out of the window in his office and noticed Karleigh had not driven away, so she must be inside of the house.

"Bingo! So, are you going to tell her?" Nick asked.

Simon was pondering whether he should say anything to Karleigh or handle the problem himself. He knew the answer; he had to tell her. She was independent and would want to control her affairs on her own. And, that's the way it should be.

"I'll tell her, but why do I feel like there is more to this story than what you are telling me?"

"We don't have all of the details just yet, but there may be more. Let's wait for my guys to get back to me." Nick told him.

Simon ended the call with Nick wondering what he should do after he told her what he knew. Would she even want his help? He was treading in unknown waters. Emotions he never had before were controlling his decisions when it came to Karleigh. He didn't want to talk to Nick about it anymore, so he called on his father.

"Dad, are you busy?" Simon asked.

"For you, Son, never. What's going on?" Simon knew his father would be available to talk.

"I have a friend that's in trouble."

"Is she pregnant?" his father flatly asked.

"Dad! Come on. No, she's not pregnant."

"But it is a woman. How is she in trouble?" Simon's father was good at getting relevant facts of information from someone. He didn't want his father to immediately know it was a woman, but he deduced that fact quickly.

"Well, it appears someone may be targeting her and discouraging her aspirations of opening a salon." Simon went on to give his father, the details of the vandalism and the information he just learned from Nick. "So, what do you think?"

"Well, Son, first, don't keep anything from her. Women don't like secrets of any kind. Even if it's in their best interest. Second, follow your heart."

"My heart? What does my heart have to do with anything?"

"Only a woman who you have feelings for would cause you to want to protect her. She must be exceptional. I can't wait to meet her."

"Thanks, Dad. Tell mom I love her, and I'll stop by sometime this week."

If his father could see through his feelings so clearly, why couldn't he make sense of them himself?

Deciding to hold on to the information until Nick got back to him, he went in search of Karleigh. He found her in his study. This particular room was dedicated to his family. A place where he could go to meditate, pray, or just be alone with his thoughts and memories. Simon kept the room private for his personal use.

Simon hadn't wanted to startle her, so he cleared his throat to get her attention. When she turned around, she did that slow-motion thing again, and her hair flowed over her shoulder. If he could, he would have melted right there on the spot. Her smile made him feel weak.

He knew right at that moment, he was in love with Karleigh. Simon would do anything to keep her safe. The need to protect her was stronger than before. The feelings were new to him, but he welcomed them with open arms.

"I assume this beautiful couple is your parents?" she asked.

Simon found it difficult to speak, so he nodded his head.

"This woman in many of the photos…is this your sister?"

"Yes," he choked up a little. "That's Sylvia. She was 22 when she passed away."

"She's beautiful. I can tell you two had a close relationship."

"She was my ace," Simon replied, then quickly changed the subject. Would you like anything to drink?"

"No, thank you. I really should be going."

Simon moved quickly to stand beside Karleigh. He wanted to get to know her better and didn't want her to leave. Finally, accepting his feelings for her, he decided to share a part of him that very few people knew.

He reached and gently grabbed her hand. They walked toward the windows in the room that faced the back of his home.

"Before you leave, I want to share something with you. You once asked me why I went into barbering. Well, it all comes back to Sylvia and my grandfather. My sister wanted horses, this house, and to own several barbershops, just like our grandfather. She saw it as a way to pay homage to our legacy. This land used to belong to my great-great-grandfather. His son sold the land to a developer and saved only these 10-acres for the family." Simon motioned to the area of land they could see from the window.

He continued. "Unbeknownst to my father and I, my grandfather and sister, had been in cahoots with one another, talking about the barbershops and this house. My grandfather died a few months after my sister. The house was almost complete. At the reading of my grandfather's will, he left me the house and the horses. The horses were supposed to be gifts for my sister."

Simon didn't release her hand. He felt her give him a little squeeze for support. "I wanted to honor both of their memories, so I quit my job in tech and opened the first barbershop. Thanks to Nick, I was able to get some high-profile clients, but I didn't really need the money. I was the primary beneficiary for my sister and my grandfather; add their life insurance payouts to the trust fund from my grandfather, and I am very well-off."

Karleigh turned to look him in the eyes. He was almost afraid to look back. Her eyes held concern and a brief flash of passion, then went immediately cold. She pulled her hand from his grasp.

"So, you didn't struggle as a new business owner?"

"I struggled. I wanted the business to do well on its own, but no, I didn't need to struggle."

"I'm over here thinking you understand what I am going through, and the whole time you are some trust-fund kid with money and playing barber for kicks and giggles."

"Listen. That's not true. Sure, I have some money, but I'm no trust fund kid. Even the money I made in Corporate America, I worked hard for. Endless days and nights. While I didn't need to struggle, I did it anyway. My only indulgences have been the cars you saw in my garage."

He had to find a way to get her to understand that he, indeed, understood her struggle. "Karleigh, I'm not trying to make light of your situation. Owning a business is never easy to start." He tried to calm his nervous body language before he continued. "I want to be a friend for you to lean on if you need to talk or need advice." He looked down for a second and then back into her eyes. "You will be successful. I believe in you."

She trembled, and Simon wanted to hold her, but he knew she wasn't ready for that. He needed to do something with his hands so he wouldn't continue to touch her. "Let me make some tea for you. You look like an herbal tea type of lady."

That evoked a chuckle from her. He was still on a rocky road with her, but at least she was smiling again.

Chapter 15

Simon hadn't had the opportunity to talk to Karleigh about Alicia. After she left his home on Sunday, he had been too busy following up on the information that Nick had given to him. Tuesday morning Simon met Karleigh at her salon when she arrived. Her hair was pulled up into a bun, showcasing her elegant facial structure. The yellow dress, paired with the oversized sunglasses, made her look like a movie star.

"Good morning, Simon. You don't want your car back already, do you?" Karleigh joked.

"No," he answered her. "Let's go inside. I need to talk to you."

Simon told Karleigh what he knew about Alicia. She didn't immediately respond, causing Simon to get a little nervous. He didn't know what she was thinking. Her calmness was disturbing.

"Are you sure it was Alicia?" she quietly asked.

"We don't have proof it was her, but her car was in the parking lot both times."

Karleigh just nodded her head. "I think I need to have a little talk with Ms. Alicia."

"Karleigh, please let the police take care of this. Nick has already contacted them and handed over all of the information he has."

She jerked her head up and stared Simon in the face. "Simon, you are not my father. If I want to go talk to Alicia, I will do just that." Karleigh angrily stood and walked away from him.

He guessed she would be angry, but he hadn't expected her to snap at him. "Listen, there is more to the story."

"Then, tell me," she barked.

Simon didn't want to tell her everything until Nick got back to him. But, he knew if he didn't, she wouldn't let it rest.

"How about we talk over breakfast. My treat." Simon was stalling for time. "We can go over to the diner you like."

He could see her considering his offer. She wasn't stupid; Karleigh knew what he was doing.

She rolled her eyes upward and responded, "I am hungry, and my first client isn't until noon. Ok, but you better tell me what in the world is going on."

She was frowning and visibly upset, he would do anything to have her smiling again. Simon wanted to fix this for her, so she wouldn't have to go through this drama as a new business owner.

They silently walked to Angelo's Delicatessen, just a few blocks from their shops. Angelo was an older gentleman from the island of Sardinia. He used to have a deli in La Maddalena when the U.S. Naval base was still operating there.

Simon ordered their food and grabbed a booth toward the back of the deli. He just needed to keep her occupied for a few more hours until the police could handle things.

When their food arrived, Karleigh didn't touch it. She sat there, sneering at Simon. He tried so hard to ignore the killer look she was giving to him and took a bite out of his California Reuben sandwich.

"Angelo makes the best California Turkey Rueben in the state," Simon said.

She continued to stare, this time tapping her fingers against the table.

"How's your sandwich?" he asked, knowing she hadn't touched it yet.

Still, she didn't say anything or divert her eyes. She added a toe tap, and Simon knew he had better say something before she exploded.

"Okay, Nick thinks Alicia may have been working with someone else to sabotage your success."

"Like who?"

"We're not sure, but maybe, Janice Carter. The owner of The Mane Event."

"Come on. Ms. Carter? Why would she want to help sabotage me? Ms. Carter doesn't even like Alicia." Karleigh finally took a bite from her sandwich, then returned it to the plate.

"Well, it was her car that was also seen in our parking lot when your car was damaged," Simon told her.

He could see the wheels in her head-turning. She was trying to sort out everything he told her. Simon knew she was processing what was being said to her when she leaned back in the booth and dropped her shoulders.

She didn't say anything for a long while. Then she grabbed her sandwich and started eating again. Simon thought that had to be a good thing. She was eating, but her silence had him worried. In the short time, he knew her; Karleigh was rarely quiet for any amount of time. He was afraid she was thinking of some sort of retaliation.

Karleigh had a client at noon, so when Simon left her at the salon, he was reasonably confident she wouldn't leave for at least an hour. That would give him time to check in with Nick, and then, he would come back and check on her.

Simon went straight to his office to call Nick. There had to be more information by now. Nick was only able to tell him that the police were going to arrest Alicia sometime during the day. It wasn't a sting operation, so the police weren't prioritizing this. They knew where she worked and would get to it when they could. That didn't sit well with Simon.

He couldn't keep Karleigh away all day. She was smart and would get suspicious real fast. He had to think of something quickly. Simon was pondering different ideas when Marquez arrived.

"Hey, Simon. Your girlfriend needs to slow down, she almost ran me over in the parking lot.

Simon jumped from his chair. "What? She's gone?"

"Yeah, she just took off like the devil, himself, was chasing her."

Quickly, Simon grabbed his keys and sprinted for the door. He had to get to her before she made it to the Mane Event. He was afraid of what she would do to Alicia when she found her.

*****

Karleigh told herself she only wanted to know why. Why would Ms. Carter be working with the likes of Alicia? But then it dawned on her…the hair show. The Mane Event had come in first-place for the last three years thanks to Karleigh and her hair creations. This would be the first year Karleigh would be attending the hair show as her own salon. But, she wasn't sure she would be entering the competition at all.

Jealousy reared its ugly head. Simon was right, this had nothing to do with the prayers she prayed. This wasn't God's doing at all. This was the devil. As she drove, Karleigh said to herself, "Devil, get thee behind me." She slowed her driving down because she recognized that she was driving like a maniac and needed to calm down before facing Alicia.

The Mane Event was decorated like a boxing ring. Ms. Carter started her hair salon in her ex-husband's boxing gym. She had won the gym in her divorce settlement and kept with the theme to make him mad. She was a vindictive woman, and that was the first indication that she could actually be jealous of Karleigh.

When Karleigh entered the salon, she was greeted by a few of the stylists that she was still friendly with. Everyone wasn't jealous of her success. However, she noticed that a few of them were a little timid and didn't engage in too much conversation. She had a funny feeling that they knew what Alicia and Ms. Carter had been up to.

She didn't bother to ask them any questions because she knew they wouldn't give her straight answers. Instead, she continued to the back of the salon, where she found Ms. Carter and Alicia huddled together. They were talking about how to block Karleigh from participating in the hair show.

"So, it's true," Karleigh stated, causing the ladies to abruptly turn around. Ms. Carter had the decency to look embarrassed.

"Who let you back here? You don't work here anymore," Alicia got in Karleigh's face.

Karleigh had a temper but was nonviolent. She took a half step back away from Alicia. She didn't want Alicia to think she could intimidate her or that she was stepping down.

"It doesn't matter who let me back here. I came here to make sense of why you would be involved with her schemes." Karleigh directed the accusation toward Ms. Carter.

"Karleigh, I didn't know she was going to vandalize your salon. I promise I would have never approved of that. But you have to understand. You were our best stylist and our best chance to win. Without you, our chances are slim."

Karleigh smiled at the off-handed compliment, and that set Alicia off. Alicia grabbed a box of powder hair bleach and tried to throw it at Karleigh. But Karleigh ducked, and it hit the wall behind her. The box burst causing a dust plume to appear. Karleigh lunged forward, trying to get to Alicia, but was restrained when someone grabbed her from the back and dragged her into the ladies' room.

Alicia started screaming at the top of her lungs because she was being held back by one of the other stylists.

Karleigh looked at herself in the mirror. This wasn't her. Fighting and carrying on. She would have never resorted to this type of behavior, but Alicia had gone too far. All for a stupid hair show that she wasn't even planning to participate in.

"Clean yourself off before you go back out there." Gee Gee had been the one to remove her from the office. She was another stylist that Karleigh really liked. "I had no idea what they were doing, but I think it's time I get out of here too. You have any booths available?" She asked, and smiled while handing a towel to Karleigh.

"I would love to have you at Serenity," Karleigh returned the smile.

Karleigh used the towel to dust her clothes and attempt to get the substance from her face and hair. Once she cleaned herself up, she held her head high and walked out of the washroom and out of the salon. *Let the police handle them.* Karleigh strutted 3 steps before she saw Simon rushing toward her.

105

Chapter 16

"Nick, meet me at the Mane Event," Simon shouted into the Bluetooth system of his car.

"Why, what's going on?"

"Karleigh may need an attorney. She was pretty mad when I told her about Alicia. She promised me she wouldn't go over there, but I'm sure that is where she is headed. I've got GPS in the Infiniti, and I'm tracking her right now. She just pulled into their parking lot."

Simon was racing down the street, trying to get to her before something happened. Nick confirmed the involvement of Ms. Carter. Apparently, Alicia was not the only person out to get Karleigh.

Everything that could happen was reeling through his mind. She could be walking into something crazy. Karleigh had no idea what she was up against. His instinctive and protective character went into overdrive, making himself crazy thinking of possible scenarios and outcomes.

Simon knew Karleigh meant a lot to him and accepted that she was his future. He could see it clearly. Everything he wanted and needed was right next door to his barbershop.

Ten minutes later, Simon arrived at The Mane Event with Nick and the police. Nick must have thought it necessary to call the police or else, why would they be there? Simon's mind, again, went to all of the horrible reasons why they would be there. He barely remembered to remove the key from the ignition before racing toward the salon.

The police were coming in right behind him. Whatever happened was over. Karleigh was heading toward him, and the ladies in the back were screaming. She smiled as she was walking toward Simon.

"What happened?" Simon asked her.

"Nothing much to tell. Ms. Alicia tried to attack me. I feel bad, I tried to lunge back at her, but I was restrained. I'll ask for forgiveness in church this week."

There was more screaming from the back as Alicia was being handcuffed, along with Ms. Carter.

"Are you okay?" Simon asked, full of concern.

She dismissed his question by waving her hand in the air. "Of course, I am. All of this trouble for a hair show."

"This was about a hair show. Women?" Nick laughed. "Hey, you two, we should meet over at Java Times. I'll tell you all about Alicia And Ms. Carter."

Chapter 17

Karleigh and Poe were sitting in the office of Serenity Hair Salon. After weeks of denying her feelings for Simon, she had to come clean. Karleigh was in love with Simon Sharpe. Everyone else knew it. At every step, since moving into the building, Simon had been there with her. Even when she hadn't wanted his help, she was glad he didn't listen to her.

"Poe, do you think I'm crazy?" she asked her sister.

"About what?" Poe was flipping through a hair magazine.

"I think I'm in love with Simon." She paused. "No. I *am* in love with Simon."

"Girl, everyone knows that," Poe replied, continuing to read the magazine.

"Is it crazy? We have known each other for what, a few months?"

"Sister, it's not crazy. Sometimes, you just know. It's easy enough to know when it's not the right person. It can be just as easy to know when you found 'the one.'" Poe used air quotes to get her point across.

Karleigh pondered what her sister had said. When you know, you just know.

They heard a commotion in the salon and jumped up to see what was happening. The scene before them was comical, to say the least. Karmyn was standing in a defensive posture, and Nick was holding his head.

"Yo, get your irrational sister. She just went kung-fu crazy on me," he yelled.

"Karmyn, what's your problem?" Karleigh asked, trying to stifle a laugh.

"He's my problem," Karmyn replied, calmly.

"I walked in here and noticed she had on headphones. I touched her shoulder, trying not to scare her and..."

"And, scared the pants out of her...I got it," Poe filled in the blank.

"When you two stop laughing, can you get me some ice? This might swell."

Poe went to the back to get the ice for Nick. Karmyn was still in her defensive stance. "Karmyn, stand down," Karleigh said, with a laugh. She then turned to Nick, "So why did you stop by here?"

"I came to invite you and your sisters..." He shot Karmyn a dirty look before continuing, "Even her...to a party, I'm having downtown at Harvest Yellow." Poe returned with the ice, handing it to Nick.

"I'm in. I love parties," Poe responded.

"Well, I can't speak for Kyna, but I'm in. Karmyn? What about you?" Karleigh knew her sister would decline, even if it weren't Nick asking.

"I can think of at least 15 other things and places I would rather be. I'm a no." Karmyn grabbed her purse. "I was leaving anyway," she said. "Goodbye, sisters." She walked passed Nick and snorted, which elicited another laugh from Karleigh and Poe.

"Good, I didn't want her to come anyway," Nick replied.

"When are you going to tell us the real story why you two hate each other," Karleigh asked.

"That's for another day and another time. Anyways, the party is this Saturday. I look forward to seeing you there." Nick took his ice and headed for the door. "Oh, and Karleigh. Simon is at his shop, waiting for you."

"Why would he be waiting for me?" Karleigh asked, puzzled.

"I figured you didn't know. He waits in the shop every night for you to leave. Making sure you are safe. Since you moved in, he has never gone home before you. And, in the days he wasn't in town, he hired security if Tyrel couldn't stay late. Goodnight, ladies."

"Well, I guess that answers that question," Poe giggled.

"What question is that?" Karleigh stood with her hands on her hips. She had no idea that Simon had been looking out for her in such a thoughtful and protective way.

"Simon is feeling you just as much as you are feeling him," Poe laughed. "Girl, you better go get your man."

*****

"You told her?" Simon slammed his bottle of soda on the countertop.

"Someone needed to get you moving. That woman will not wait on you forever," Nick sat in Marquez chair, scrolling through emails on his phone.

Simon was angry and thankful at the same time. If Nick hadn't told her, he might not have ever brought it up. Knowing Karleigh like he does, she would get upset.

"I also invited them to the party Saturday," Nick said

"Really, them? Her sisters too?"

"Yep, Karleigh and her fine sisters."

"Including Karmyn?" Simon asked, knowing it would get a reaction from him.

"Yeah, well, I couldn't not invite her. She declined anyway."

Simon thought he knew about all of Nick's escapades. But his situation with Karmyn was still a mystery to himself and Karleigh's sisters.

"Are you ever going to tell me what's up between you two?" Simon asked.

"Nothing to tell, she hates me, case-closed." Nick stood, stretching his lean body. "I'm heading out to meet with my event planner."

Simon was left with his thoughts yet again. Knowing Karleigh was aware that he had been staying late, watching after her, he wondered what she was thinking. Since he finally came to terms with his feelings, he didn't care that she knew. It wouldn't stop him from staying late at night and waiting for her.

After an hour, he watched Karleigh and her sister leave the salon. Only this time, they both looked over to his barbershop and waved goodbye.

Simon's heart took a dip, knowing she was upset with him. He smiled waved back and went to set his alarm. Walking toward his car, he received a text message from Karleigh.

THANKS

Chapter 18

Nick had talked Simon into some crazy things since college, but this one had to top them all. Harvest Yellow was code for a barn party. Like, an actual barn with haystacks, live animals, and a mechanical bull. Harvest Yellow meant corn, and all the food and drinks had corn or the word yellow in their names.

Simon walked over to the bartender who was wearing overalls and a straw hat, read the menu, and asked for the Flint corn drink, which was made with Mountain Dew, vodka, and grenadine. The sugary concoction was served in a cup designed like a half ear of corn. Simon thought this had to be the weirdest place for the upscale, fine-dining attorney Nicolas Butler to host a party.

The dance floor was packed, and everyone seemed to know the Boot-Scootin Boogie by Brooks and Dunn. Simon spotted Karleigh, and her sisters come in through the main barn doors. All four of them expressed shock when they entered, just as he had. He was glad he wasn't the only one who didn't expect this scene from Nick.

He grabbed his drink from the bar and quickly walked over toward the sisters. The first sip of his Flint corn drink had him gagging and spewing the contents from his mouth onto Karleigh.

"Oh my goodness, Karleigh. I'm so sorry." He took his napkin and tried to wipe her off. "This drink is more sugary than I thought. And, the taste is disgusting." Her silence made him feel more embarrassed. But, at least she wasn't looking angry.

"It's okay, Simon," she finally said. "I'll just go to the ladies' room and clean up a little."

"Sister, I have an extra shirt in my car. I'll go get it," Poe offered.

Simon watched the two sisters walk away in different directions.

"Smooth. Very smooth," Kyna laughed. "I'm heading to the bar." She walked away, leaving Karmyn and Simon alone.

"What made you decide to attend?" he asked Karmyn.

"I didn't want to. I was asked by a client of mine." Karmyn's statement held a measure of annoyance.

Simon wasn't getting good vibes from Karmyn. There was usually a softness under her tough exterior. She played hardcore, but deep down, Simon would bet she was a marshmallow. He wanted to ask her another question but was interrupted by the ringing of her cell phone.

"I'm going to step outside to take this call, in case my sisters ask." Karmyn walked away, leaving him standing alone.

Simon remained by the door, hoping Karleigh would return soon. He felt kind of awkward and out of place dressed up for a fancy party among the city's country-western scene. As soon as he found Nick, he was going to wring his neck for not telling him.

Simon kept looking around while waiting for Karleigh to return. He spotted a few of his friends and clients on the dance floor and around the barn. The DJ was doing an excellent job of mixing country and club music to keep people on the dance floor. Simon had yet to see Nick at his own party.

Within a few minutes, Karleigh and Poe returned and flanked Simon. They were both smiling, that was a good sign. He definitely didn't want Karleigh or her sisters upset with him for any reason. Especially as he was still trying to build his courage to ask Karleigh to move their friendship to relationship status.

Simon was just about to ask Karleigh if she wanted something to drink. His back was turned to the mechanical bull and never saw the cowboy boot that knocked him upside the head, knocking him off his feet, rendering him dazed and confused.

*****

The DJ stopped playing music, and a crowd quickly formed around them.

"Oh My God, Simon, say something!" Karleigh was on her knees, cradling Simon's head in her lap. "Kyna, quick, what am I supposed to do?"

Kyna couldn't stop laughing. Between outbursts, she managed to check his pulse. "He's not even unconscious."

"What happened?" Simon fluttered his eyelids.

"You were hit with a boot," Karleigh tried to stifle her laughter.

"What was in the boot, lead?" Simon asked, rubbing the back of his head.

"Kyna, seriously, do something," Karleigh yelled at her sister.

Kyna kneeled beside him. "Okay, remember these three words…tree, father, shotgun. Do you know where you are?"

"Yeah, a stupid barn party." Simon was going to kill Nick when he saw him.

"Good, what did you have to drink?" Kyna asked, laughing through the question.

"A syrupy corn drink that was horrible." Simon continued rubbing his head, feeling a knot begin to form.

"Awesome, last question. What's your middle name?"

Simon wouldn't typically answer this question, but without a second thought, he blurted out, "Cleodis."

Everyone standing around roared, "CLEODIS!"

After the laughter subsided, Karleigh helped him to his feet. "Are you going to be okay?"

"Yeah, I guess," Simon replied.

Kyna helped to support his other side, allowing Simon to shift his weight between the two sisters. "What were the three words I asked you to remember?" she asked.

"Tree, father, and shotgun," he answered.

"Good. Remember those words if you do anything to hurt my sister." Kyna gave him an unsmiling stare and shrugged his arm away from her shoulder. She walked away toward the dance floor.

The Hammond sisters were going to be the death of him, either physically or from a broken heart. She might not know it, but Karleigh had the power to rip his heart to shreds.

Nick rushed over and tried to disperse the crowd. "Nothing to see here, folks. Let's keep the party going." When the DJ started up again, the group started to thin out. Nick turned to Karleigh. "Let's help him over to the VIP section so he can sit down," he suggested.

The VIP section had a few haystacks that served as sitting, and a couple of hard plastic chairs roped off near the bar. Karleigh and Nick helped Simon onto the first empty sofa making sure to be gentle with him. Karleigh didn't want to believe Simon was just playing along, but she caught him, giving Nick a wink of the eye. So, when she got to the sofa, she flung his arm a little too forcefully, causing Simon to go off-balance and lose his footing, again, hitting the floor.

"Bro, you sure you want to be in this abusive relationship?" Nick jokingly asked before leaving them alone.

Karleigh cut her eyes at Simon. He was truly unbelievable. She wanted to be mad at him, but she couldn't. Through the mishaps in just one night, he was still trying to be cool. She figured she would make this awkward situation of theirs a little more comfortable.

"You know, if you want me to hold you, next time you should just ask," Karleigh smiled.

"Really?" Simon responded in a high-pitched voice. Deciding it was too high, he deepened his voice to repeat it. "Really?"

"Simon, I like you. A lot. You've done some really nice things for me since opening my salon. I didn't want to feel needy, but I do appreciate everything that you have done." Karleigh paused and fidgeted with her hands. She wasn't as self-assured as she portrayed. She felt his hands on hers and looked up into his beautiful brown eyes.

Speaking at the same time, they said., "Would you like to go out?"

Realizing that they had asked each other the same question, they began laughing hysterically.

On the other side of the room, unknown to the group, a beautiful woman held her cell phone up, took a picture of Simon and Karleigh, and quickly sent it to her bosses. The accompanying text: *Mission Accomplished.*

Chapter 19

Date night finally arrived, Karleigh would be going on her first official date with Simon. Coffee from time to time didn't qualify as a real date. She was more nervous now than when she quit her job to go to cosmetology school. Poe and Karmyn were on the way over to her house to help her prepare.

Every few minutes, Karleigh tried to talk herself out of going, and then she asked herself, why not? Why shouldn't she go on a date with Simon? Because she wasn't his type of woman, she tried to tell herself. But Karleigh didn't know what his kind of woman was.

Over the past few months, Karleigh tried not to pay too much attention to Simon, but she couldn't stop. He was always in her space, doing something thoughtful, helping her with her salon, loaning her a car. Men in her world just didn't do these things, yet Simon did.

Karleigh still believed Simon had an ulterior motive, and she needed to know why. Before they could go any further in this relationship, questions needed to be asked, and answers had to be given. Thinking about the word relationship, she wondered if that was what they had? She would find out soon enough.

Her doorbell rang, indicating her sisters had arrived. She desperately needed them to help calm her nerves. Karleigh quickly raced to the door and swung it open. "I thought you would never get here."

"I didn't know you were expecting me. I'm really early."

"AAAHHHH!" Karleigh slammed the door in Simon's face. She was only dressed in her robe and slippers with the raccoon faces. "What are you doing here?" she yelled through the door.

Trying to stifle a laugh, Simon replied, "We need to talk. I found out some interesting news."

"Well, I'm not presentable. Come back in three hours."

Simon laughed, "I'm here now, and you look fine. Please let me in."

"I'll open this door, but I need to get dressed. Wait 10 seconds, then come in. And WAIT in the living room." She unlocked the door and quickly ran into her bedroom. Embarrassment didn't adequately describe how she felt. Add shock and humiliation.

Karleigh searched her room for something to throw on. Everything she pulled out was not appropriate to wear around him. She finally found a University of Michigan t-shirt and some jeans that were a little baggier on her than she liked.

When she entered the living room, Simon was sitting on her sofa, looking very comfortable. He didn't appear out of place, and that made Karleigh feel anxious. She had never had any men, other than family, in her home. Yet, Simon eased right in.

"Okay, so what's going on?" she sat on the sofa, opposite of Simon.

His eyes were intense and made Karleigh feel slightly uneasy. She shifted on the sofa and placed her feet underneath her to get more comfortable.

"I found out some interesting information today from Ms. Norma," Simon started to tell her.

"Mr. Dorsey's secretary? What did she say?"

Before Simon could speak, the doorbell rang. Karleigh excused herself and went to the door. Poe entered with her arms full of bags.

"Sister, I am ready to turn you into a goddess for Simon. When I'm done with you, his heart will stop, and you will have to perform CPR."

"Poe!" Karleigh tried to admonish her sister.

"Hi Poe," Simon said casually from the living room.

"Oh. Whoa! Simon, what are you doing here? Your date isn't for another four hours." Poe checked her watch.

"Simon stopped by early to discuss a business matter with me."

Poe didn't appear to believe Karleigh, and she kept eyeing Simon suspiciously. "Well, are you two still going out?"

"I hope so," Simon answered.

Poe grabbed her bags, again, and started walking toward Karleigh's bedroom. "I will just take these things in the back and wait for you."

Karleigh tried to remain in control and not show Simon she was feeling anxious. She had so many questions and no answers.

"Okay, what did Ms. Norma tell you?" she returned to the sofa.

"It seems as if the Dorsey brothers have been keeping secrets. Our building…" Simon was interrupted by the doorbell again.

"I'm sorry. I bet that is Karmyn. My sisters were coming over to help me get ready."

"I see." Simon gave her a smile that made her skin tingle.

Karleigh went to the door, and just like Poe, Karmyn started talking before Karleigh could warn her they were not alone.

"Sister, I stopped by Victoria's Secret and picked up some lady items. You never know what could happen. You need to be prepared."

Karleigh wanted to fall through a hole in the floor and escape the constant humiliation she felt. She didn't even look over to Simon. She knew he was inwardly laughing.

"Hi, Karmyn," Simon said in the same low, gravelly voice.

"Simon! What are you doing here?" Karmyn asked.

"He has some business to talk to me about. Yes, we are still going out, and Poe is in my room, where you are going right now." Karleigh pushed her sister toward her bedroom.

This time when she returned, Simon was standing in her kitchen.

"I'm so sorry. Would you like something to drink? I have juice, wine and water," she said.

Simon grabbed her hand and pulled her further into the kitchen, out of the line of sight of her sisters who were peering from behind the bedroom door, and far enough where they couldn't be heard,

"Before I get back to business, I need to do this," Simon kissed her with an almighty passion.

*****

Simon didn't know what had come over him. He hadn't planned to take her in her own kitchen and assault her with a passionate kiss, but he couldn't help it. Knowing she enlisted the help of her sisters to prepare for their date did something to him. It was endearing and made him feel special. He was appreciative that she would go to the trouble to look even more beautiful for him.

He used his free hand to tip her chin upward, forcing her to look at him. "Karleigh, I am trying to understand this attraction I have to you. I like you a lot." He looked down, took a deep breath, and then look back up into her beautiful brown eyes. "I more than like you. I love you."

He wasn't ready for the tears that escaped her eyes or the tremble he felt through her hands. Simon used the back of his thumb to wipe away the tears from her cheek.

"Simon, I love you, too. I tried to talk myself out of it. We haven't known each other long, but I feel it. I was so afraid that you were doing these things for me for other reasons. I don't know, I always seem to jump to conclusions, and they are usually wrong."

From the other room, Poe screamed, "And, you talk too much! Geesh."

Simon and Karleigh both laughed. It felt good to know that Karleigh felt the same way about him. He led her back to the living room sofa. This time he made sure she sat right next to him. He then asked Karmyn and Poe to join them.

"I found out that the Dorsey's are selling our building to an investor within the next few months. And the new investors want to tear the building down."

Karleigh jumped up. "They can't do that. I just signed my lease."

Simon grabbed her hand and gently tugged her back down beside him.

"Yes, they can. And, not only that, the new building owners do not have to resign our leases when they end."

Tears began forming in Karleigh's eyes again. This time they weren't because of good news.

"So, how much is the building?" Karmyn asked.

"From what I heard, they are listing it for $1.2 million."

Karmyn and Poe both let out a slow breath. Karleigh's tears were refreshed and flowing more freely now. He knew that Karleigh was thinking of the worst-case scenarios. Simon gently tugged her hand to get Karleigh to look at him.

"Hey, this is not the end of Serenity. We will work through this."

Poe moved closer to the couple. "Sister, beauty is your passion," she said. "Do not lose your faith in your passion and purpose now. So, you are facing some type of adversity. I know God has a plan for you. A plan to prosper you and not harm you, plans to give you hope and a future."

Simon knew that scripture very well, Jeremiah 29:11 (NIV), and he had to agree with Poe. She was very spiritual and knew what to say and when to say it. Her words were also meant for him. His own faith in his future had wavered when he found out about the sale of the building.

He was still holding Karleigh's hand while she sat there, not saying anything. He didn't know what to do or say next. The moment was awkward for him and her sisters. Finally, Karmyn spoke up.

"So, are you two still going to dinner? If not, I can make something from this pitiful refrigerator of Karleigh's."

That garnered a laugh from Karleigh and Poe. Simon guessed that it was an inside joke about Karleigh's refrigerator. After taking a look for himself, he realized Karleigh didn't do much cooking for herself.

Their first date would be put on hold as they all put their heads together to discuss their options if the building were to get sold. Karleigh had a lease for another nine months. Simon's contract was due to expire in less than six months.

Chapter 20

Karleigh and Simon had been trying to have their first official date for over a month. Every time they both had the time, something would always come up. Simon desperately wanted to wine and dine her, but they settled for a quick coffee before opening or lunch in one of their offices.

The barbershop was quiet for a Thursday afternoon. Simon had just finished balancing the books for the month and was about to head out for the day. There was an Arabian pure-breed stallion that was being auctioned, and he wanted to take a look at her.

The light chatter of the shop all ceased when he left his office and entered the main room.

"Okay, what's going on out here? You guys are up to something," he said.

No one said anything. Marquez rotated his chair, turning his back to Simon. Tyrel looked up, smiled, and then back down to the customer in his chair. Roxanne never once made any acknowledgment that Simon had asked a question.

"Now, I'm getting concerned. Somebody better start talking," Simon deepened his voice to sound more authoritative.

"Men, ugh! Your girlfriend next door just left. Asking all these questions about you. What you like to do in your spare time, what's your favorite color. I mean, she should know, not us."

"Oh, really!?" Simon was intrigued. "Well, let me get over there and find out what's going on."

The air outside was stifling hot. A smothering of sorts. The humidity was thick and made it hard to breathe. Simon walked toward Serenity and noticed a man dressed in all black standing near the light in the parking lot. The stranger wore a black ball cap and long sleeves.

When they made eye contact, the guy turned quickly and walked off. Simon watched him until he turned the corner and out of sight. He seemed out of place and put Simon on edge.

The air from Serenity blasted Simon in the face, and he was able to take a full, deep breath. Nothing appeared out of place. Gee Gee and Jasmine were at their stations, chatting away with their clients. The radio was lightly playing in the background. He assumed Karleigh was in her office.

"Hello, ladies."

"Hey, Simon. Karleigh's not here."

"What do you mean? She was just at my shop, and her car is outside."

"She never came back from visiting you. We thought she was still there."

Simon's mind went into overdrive. Taking his phone from his pocket, he tried to call her. The call went straight to voicemail. She had to be within walking distance. Back outside, the humidity overwhelmed him again.

Scanning the parking lot, he didn't see anything out of the ordinary. Across the street, he spotted the stranger in all black again. This time, he was smoking a cigarette, leaning against the side of the bakery.

Simon moved to hide behind a column in front of his building and watched the stranger. After a few minutes, he saw Karleigh exit the bakery and walk to the corner of the intersection to cross the street. He was thankful that she didn't try to pass in the middle of traffic.

The stranger followed slowly behind Karleigh. From a distance, Simon kept his eyes on both of them. She was getting closer to Serenity, and the stranger sped up his walking.

Karleigh suddenly stopped and reached into her purse, allowing the stranger to close the distance. Simon stepped out into the parking lot, ready to take on the stranger if he needed to. Then, it happened so fast, Karleigh quickly spun on her heels and sprayed the stranger with pepper spray.

The stranger stumbled backward and tripped, falling to the pavement. Simon was calling 911 when he approached. The smell of the pepper spray and the humidity caused them all to start choking.

"Karleigh! Stop spraying that stuff." He managed to say between coughs.

"He has been following me all day," she said, as she leaned over the stranger. "You think I'm stupid? You think I didn't see you? I ought to hit you with the stun gun!" she screamed angrily.

Simon felt instantly proud of her. She was ready to defend herself and wasn't afraid to do so. More bonus points for Karleigh. He was able to restrain the stranger while they waited for assistance.

Tyrel heard the commotion outside and came to assist Simon to keep the stranger under control. They let him sit and suffer through the pepper spray until the paramedics arrived.

The police took the stranger into custody for questioning. Unfortunately, there wasn't much else the police could do. The man had not said or done anything to Karleigh, he was just walking behind her. It's a misdemeanor of stalking or intimidation at best. Later, Nick showed up with more information and was able to find out the stranger was the brother of Alicia. He was planning to rob and scare Karleigh.

"All of this over a hair show," Karleigh said.

"People do the craziest things for money," Nick replied.

"What money? The hair show is just for bragging rights. Right?" Karleigh was suddenly unsure.

"Karleigh, there is a $5,000 cash prize for the top stylist this year. And, an additional $5,000 for the salon with the top-scored stylists," Simon answered her.

*****

Later that evening Karleigh was still shocked. She was feeling hurt and confused, but the strongest emotion was betrayed. She couldn't believe that Ms. Carter or Alicia would go to this much trouble. The cash prizes explained everything now. Karleigh jumped to her laptop and pulled up the information for the hair show. She could possibly win up to $10,000 for the salon. She would be able to bank that money and pay off her loans or make a down payment on purchasing the building herself.

"What is going on in that pretty head of yours? I see the wheels turning." Simon had entered her office, handing her a drink, and taking a seat in front of her desk.

"I think that if I enter the hair show this year, I could win the money I need to either pay off my loans or make an investment and purchase this building myself. I wouldn't have to move, you wouldn't have to move. It's a win-win."

"Actually, I've been thinking about that. I have enough in investments to liquidate a sizeable down payment on the building. I thought we could become business partners."

"Business partners? You and me?" Karleigh wasn't sure about that arrangement. Dating was one thing, but being tied to him in a business partnership could be tricky.

"Yeah, what's the problem?" Simon leaned back in the chair, watching her for a reaction.

"Haven't you ever heard, you shouldn't mix business and pleasure?"

"Well, we have yet to go on our first date. So, there is no mixing yet," Simon challenged.

Karleigh watched Simon move closer to her. He was stalking her like a preying cat. Their eyes remained connected until the intense moment was broken when Poe entered her office.

"Did I interrupt something?" Poe asked.

"Yes," Simon answered.

"No," Karleigh countered. "What's up, sister?"

"I just stopped by to see if you wanted to get lunch."

Karleigh gave Simon her best sympathetic look. "Sure."

"Simon, you can come, too," Poe invited him.

"No, thanks. I think I will just go to my office. I have a few clients this evening," Simon sounded defeated.

Karleigh and Poe remained in her office after Simon left. She filled her sister in on the latest drama with Alicia and the cash prize for the hair show.

"Oh my God, sister, that money is just what you need. Didn't I tell you God would work it out."

"I haven't won the hair show yet, sister."

"But saying yet, means you are going to enter," Poe said excitedly.

"I think I am, but I need to get Gee Gee and Jasmine on board with the idea to compete as a salon."

Karleigh and Poe waited until all of the clients had gone before meeting with her stylists. After telling them about the situation that occurred, and the hair show, both stylists, agreed to compete. That was all they needed to begin the planning process.

Poe had ordered everyone sandwiches from Angelo's while they talked business. A while later, Poe had to take care of some business and left, along with Jasmine's drop-in customer, when a young lady entered. She wasn't a customer and appeared apprehensive when she approached.

"May I help you?" Karleigh asked.

"Uhhhh, I'm looking for the salon owner." She looked down at a piece of paper in her hand. "Her name is Karleigh Hammond."

"I'm Karleigh. How can I help you?"

"My name is Shelina. My grandmother, Norma Jean Hansberry, said that I may be able to rent a booth here. I'm a hairstylist from Chicago."

Jasmine looked at Karleigh, who then looked at Gee Gee; all three of them had a look of amazement. The moment was like divine intervention. They would have been okay entering the competition with three stylists, but four made it better.

"Hi, Shelina. Come on in. Your grandmother is correct; I have some booths for rent." She showed the young lady to an empty booth. "Do you have any experience?"

"I have my portfolio, and my social media account has some of my previous clients."

Karleigh took the small photo book from Shelina and started flipping through the photos. Jasmine and Gee Gee went to social media to look at her pictures.

"Girl, you are amazing. Why'd you leave Chicago?" Gee Gee asked.

"It was time for something new. And, before you ask, it has nothing to do with a man or anything. I was just ready to grow somewhere else."

Karleigh gave Gee Gee a stern look as she said, "Your reason for relocating is really none of our business. But, I agree, you are really talented. How do you feel about competitions?" Shelina's pictures were amazing. The hairstyles ranged from classic to innovative. That was a plus for the hair show.

"Competitions? You mean against each other, or at a hair show?" Shelina seemed nervous.

"A hair show," all three women responded.

"I've never been in a hair show competition before."

"If you're interested, we are entering as a salon and would love to have you on board."

The four women talked for over an hour, getting to know Shelina better, and more about the hair show. They were determined to put Serenity Salon and Spa on the map and win the money to purchase the building. Karleigh had faith in the team God put together for her.

Chapter 21

In preparation for the hair show, Karleigh had been so busy, she hadn't seen Simon but a few times in passing. Her car insurance company totaled her car, so she was still driving Simon's Infiniti. She tried to give it back, but he wouldn't hear of it.

She was sitting in her office, trying to recall the last time she shared a meal with Simon. It had been weeks, they both were busy with their own businesses. Her sisters didn't even come by the salon as often as they used to. Karmyn was always working at her gym, Poe had gained some very demanding corporate clients, and Kyna was being Kyna.

The hair show was in two weeks, and Gee Gee and Jasmine had their client's styles ready to go. They were still working with Shelina on her clients. Since she was new, she was still building clientele to work from. She currently had three regulars, and they were older ladies from the church.

Karleigh had asked almost every woman she knew to participate. Only able to secure two models for Shelina, but they needed two more. She dropped her head into her hands and closed her eyes. "Lord, if this is your will."

In perfect timing, the door opened and in walked Roxanne.

"Hey, Roxy, what's up?" Karleigh asked.

"I heard you were entering the hair show."

"Yeah, you heard right."

"Well, I want in. Simon doesn't enter, and I thought that maybe I could be of some help. I know you trying to win the prize for your salon. So, count me in."

Karleigh was taken aback. She didn't think Roxanne liked her at all. Most days, she didn't say hello or even acknowledge her in passing. Karleigh felt like she didn't exist to Roxanne.

"Did Simon talk to you?" Karleigh asked her.

"No, he didn't have to. Actually, I need to get my name out there and increase my brand."

Karleigh didn't need to think about it. Adding a barber who was also a loctician to her team would be the icing on the cake she needed to put them over the top. "Welcome aboard."

*****

The day of the hair show was frantic, with over 200 stylists representing over 100 salons, from 8 different states. Women and men were setting up their individual areas. Stylists were required to complete more than 50% of their styles on their live models in the open space.

Hair extensions were flying across the room, hair spray thickened the air, and the music was pumping loudly. The scene was pure comedy for those who had never attended a hair show and competition.

Karleigh arrived at the show after Gee Gee and Jasmine. That familiar feeling of dread crept into her mind as she approached their assigned booth. She recognized that something was wrong when she saw Jasmine's face.

"What's wrong?" Karleigh asked, going into panic mode.

"They put us next to The Mane Event," Jasmine nodded her head to the right. "And we only have three styling chairs."

"What? We need five styling chairs, what are we supposed to do?" Karleigh had to take deep breaths to maintain her composure. Again, it was feeling like God was trying to tell her something.

"Honestly, I think they took one of our chairs." Gee Gee pointed to the booth where the stylists from The Mane Event were setting up.

"Okay, let's not panic. I can use a regular chair, and my styles won't take too long. My models were prepped last night. What about you two?"

"I have two models that will need some additional time," Jasmine answered.

"I'm okay, I can do mine standing if I need to," Gee Gee added.

"Okay, Good. I know Roxy will need a chair. I only need to check on Shelina." Karleigh was pacing the floor.

Within the hour, Roxy and Shelina arrived at their station. They were briefed on the minor situation with The Mane Event. Gee Gee had to use her strength to physically restrain Roxy from jumping over the divider to confront Alicia and the other stylists. Shelina was able to adapt quickly to her lack of equipment, and like Karleigh thought she could work without a chair.

The hair show competition consisted of fabulous hairstyles, creative themes, and performances, including dancing, acting, and modeling. The judges were looking for diversity, creativity, and innovation. During the first round, the judges observe the stylists preparing their models. The second phase of the competition is when the real entertainment begins.

Karleigh was exhausted after styling her models for the past six hours. The other models were also styled and dressed on time. Jasmine was finishing the make-up on her last model when Alicia strolled in front of their section. She should have been in jail, but one of her clients is a really good attorney.

"Don't engage. Don't engage," Karleigh whispered to her stylists.

"Is there something you need?" Gee Gee asked when Alicia stood in front of them without saying a word.

"There is a word for a person like you." Directing her comment to Gee Gee. "Traitor is one of them," Alicia finally said.

"It's more like integrity. In case you're not sure what that means, let me tell you. Doing the right thing, even when no one is watching."

"Good for you, girl scout." Alicia looked around the area. "Good luck," she said as she walked away.

Simon, Nick, and Poe were approaching Karleigh as Alicia was walking away. Simon knew that the interaction with Alicia wasn't good and went immediately to Karleigh. She was scowling and visibly shaken by Alicia's appearance.

"Hey, you okay?" Simon grabbed her hands and pulled her close to him.

"She really knows how to get under my skin," Karleigh was on the verge of tears. She was so angry.

Simon rubbed his hands up and down her arms to comfort her. "Why don't you sit down, we have something to tell you."

"What now?" Karleigh couldn't take anymore. She was hanging onto her last thread of sanity.

"Poe found out our building has been sold."

"What? How?" That did it. Karleigh heard the thread snap, and she felt like she was free-falling in a bottomless pit. Murphy's Law was slapping her across the face.

"Sister, when you told me about the Dorsey's selling the building, I started keeping an eye on commercial investors. This morning, an offer was made and accepted," Poe informed her.

"Do you know who?" Karleigh asked.

"It's being kept a secret. All we know is there will be new owners," Nick added.

"I'm sorry, sister," Poe expressed her regret.

"But what does this really mean? I'm only 6-months into a one-year lease. The Dorsey brothers gave me an option to sign for longer if my business took off. We are taking off, and now I may have to move. This is crazy."

"Faith. Keep your faith. This is the time when you are supposed to have crazy faith. You started your business, overcame obstacles, increased your clientele, and have more stylists, all with crazy faith. Don't stop now," Simon told her.

Karleigh knew he was right. Her faith had brought her this far, and it would take her even further. "You're right. I have crazy faith," she said, wiping her tears away. "God has a plan for me, and I have to trust what it is." She stood and faced her stylists and announced, "We are going into this hair show to win and then take each day one at a time."

"That's my girl," Simon pulled her into a comfortable embrace.

"Am I? Your girl?" she whispered for his ears only.

"You've always been my girl. I love you, Karleigh," he whispered back.

Karleigh took his words of love and mixed them in the pot with his support and her feelings for him; that gave her all the strength she needed to move forward. With Simon by her side, she knew she would be able to handle anything. She smiled but didn't say anything.

"After you rock this hair show, I promise to take you on our first real date," Simon said.

*****

Simon was impressed and proud of Serenity Hair Salon and Spa. They had stayed true to their beliefs and went with an ethereal performance. Each of the models was dressed in a unique all-white evening gown and a pair of angel wings. They were reminiscent of Victoria's Secret models. Karleigh went with a custom remix of gospel singer Erica Campbell's "I Luh God" and Tye Tribbett's "Work It Out."

Serenity's performance had everyone on their feet dancing. The crowd went crazy when Shelina's children's styles hit the stage, and they performed a choreographed dance. This was the most excited Simon had ever been at one of these hair shows.

They had to sit through 22 salon performances. Each with their own unique flair. The waiting for the judges to tally their scores was getting nerve-wracking, and Simon could see Karleigh trying to keep it together. She was nervous about the results but also worried about the new building owners.

If he admitted the truth, he too was concerned. Had he known earlier that the Dorsey brothers were going to sell the building, he would have bought it himself. Not only concerned about his future, but he cared about his barbers and Karleigh. His other barbershops could absorb his barbers, but that would be an inconvenience to them and their clients. That also left no neighborhood barbershop in the area for the kids.

Simon needed to listen to his own words of encouragement and have faith. He wasn't going to try and understand God's plan, just remember that He had an idea for both of them.

While the judges continued their deliberation, Simon held Karleigh's hand and lowered his head. He closed his eyes and began to pray. Simon prayed for guidance, strength, and security for their future. What he didn't pray for was to win the competition. Karleigh didn't need to win to know she was highly favored. He would spend his days making sure she knew she was loved.

When he finished his prayer, a chorus of amens was heard around him. Serenity stylists, his barbers, and the Hammond sisters had circled them. Covered and protected them with their love.

From a distance, a woman was watching the spiritual scene. She sent a text to her bosses. *Closer and closer,* it read.

The judges approached the stage along with the announcer. The results were in. In third place was Nouveau Hair Studio, and second place went to Jasper's Hair Depot. They anxiously awaited the announcement for the first-place winner. Simon felt the pressure of Karleigh's grip increasing.

"Baby, no matter what happens, you are talented, and I am very proud of you."

"Thank you," she whispered and wiped away a single tear that escaped from her eye.

"And, the grand prize winner of $5,000 and a photo-shoot for Nubian Magazine is…Oh my God, I can't believe it. The winner is newcomer Serenity Salon and Spa! Ms. Karleigh Hammond, get yourself up here, girl," the announcer said.

Simon walked Karleigh toward the stage to receive her award. But they were stopped a few feet short of the steps. Alicia had blocked their path full of rage and venom.

"Stop right there! I demand a recount. There is no way The Mane Event didn't at least place," Alicia shouted.

The announcer shouted into the microphone for the entire convention hall to hear, "Honey, The Mane Event used yesteryear's hairstyles with last year's fashion. The only thing y'all winning is the 'recycle your style' fashion show." He pushed her to one side and allowed Simon and Karleigh to take the stage.

Alicia wasn't finished with her tirade and attempted to take the stage. Roxy grabbed her by the ponytail and pulled her backward. Unbeknownst to Roxy, the ponytail wasn't secured tightly when she pulled, and the hair went flying into the air.

The ponytail hairpiece hit a gentleman across the room in the face causing the crowd to laugh hysterically. Alicia was angry and embarrassed. She ran away, trying to cover her head with her hands.

Simon stared at Alicia's retreating back as she ran away. The woman was unbelievable and deserved everything to come her way. Karleigh tried her best not to laugh, but couldn't hold it in as others around the stage continued laughing while the stylist from The Mane Event exited the venue.

After the hair show, there was an after-party at the host hotel that Karleigh and her stylists, friends, and family were attending. Several local celebrities were also in attendance, including a few of Simon's and Nick's clients. Simon was shocked that Nick and Karmyn were able to sit within 10 feet of each other and not commit murder.

Simon secured a section in the VIP area with bottle service for everyone in their group. He was happy to see Tyrel come out to celebrate with Karleigh. Since Gee Gee came to Serenity, he noticed Tyrel stayed hanging around a lot more often.

The waitress came over to deliver two bottles of champagne. Simon wanted to toast to Karleigh and her success. Nick filled everyone's glass as Simon stood, preparing to give his speech.

"Today, we celebrate Serenity Salon and Spa for their amazing accomplishment. Karleigh had a vision, she had her friends and family to support her, and with crazy faith, she proved nothing is impossible. There is nothing, and I mean nothing that can stand in her way. I am so happy that God put her in my life. To Serenity."

"To Serenity!" everyone shouted.

It was a near-perfect evening, but Simon had one last thing to do. He contemplated asking her in front of her family and friends but decided against it. His ego was fragile and couldn't sustain rejection from her. Especially after he told her he loved her. He needed to be alone when he asked her.

Simon followed Karleigh home after the party. She was still driving his car, and as far as he was concerned, she could keep it if she wanted to.

Anything she wanted, Simon would move mountains if she needed him to. He parked his car in her driveway and waited for her to exit her vehicle.

"Thanks for following me home, Simon," she said.

"Did you enjoy yourself today?" he asked.

"It's been a super long day, but it was well worth it." She finished with a big yawn. "I didn't think I was that tired, but I guess I am. Will I see you at church tomorrow?"

And just like that, he was afraid to ask his question. His nerves were frayed even though he didn't outwardly show it.

"Sure, would you like for me to pick you up in the morning?"

"I would love it, thank you. You know that means you are expected to come to dinner at my parents."

"I know." He moved in closer to her. She had opened the door and turned off the alarm. When she turned around, Simon was right next to her. "I just wanted to tell you, I am very proud of you. Goodnight." He placed the softest kiss on her cheek and returned to his car.

If he stayed any longer or kissed her on the lips, he was sure to throw away all of his Christian values. He had to get home quickly and pray for continued strength.

But rather than go home, Simon sat in his car for about ten minutes. This was crazy. She had said she loved him, too. This shouldn't be so hard. Simon went back and forth in his mind of what to do next. Then he heard a voice, clear as day. The voice simply said, "Now."

Simon took a deep breath, slowly released the air from his lungs, and marched right back to Karleigh's front door. He knocked three times, hoping she was still awake.

"It's now or never," Simon whispered to himself.

The door swung open, and Karleigh stood there looking ever-so beautiful. The lighting behind her made her appear delicate and soft. She was still wearing her dress from the hair show, but she had let her hair down, and the curls bounced around her shoulders.

"Did you forget something?" she asked.

Simon couldn't get the words out. He was stuttering and stumbling, trying to say something. Tripping over his words was becoming embarrassing for both of them. He was finally able to regain his composure and asked to enter.

"Come on in. Would you like something to drink?"

"No," he grabbed her hand to turn her around. He slowly descended to one knee in her hallway. Right here, right now, he was going to do it. "Karleigh, this will be the third time I say this to you. I love you."

She tried to pull her hand away, but Simon wouldn't let go. She used her other hand to cover her mouth.

"Karleigh, the past six months have been crazy, even with the way you came into my life. I knew then you were special. You made me nervous, just being around you. And now, I can't imagine my life without you."

Karleigh was in full-blown sobs now. He couldn't tell if she was happy or not, but he forged on, hoping for the best. A three-carat diamond solitaire was on his pinky finger. He slid it from his hand to hers and gazed into her eyes. "Karleigh, will you marry me?"

She didn't say anything at first. Simon was preparing for the rejection. Even if she said no, he wouldn't give up on her.

Through her tears, she started shaking her head and finally said, "yes." Simon barely heard her whisper.

He flashed his million-dollar smile. "I didn't hear you. Can you say it again?"

This time when he asked, she screamed, "Yes! Yes!"

Chapter 22

Luke 12:34 For where your treasure is, there your heart will be also.

Neither of them got much sleep. After Karleigh said yes, they prayed and talked for a brief time, mostly about how Sunday morning would go. They would be attending church together, and she would be wearing her ring.

Strangely, Karleigh didn't feel nervous at all. She was excited. Her sisters would be just as thrilled. She only worried about her grandmother's reaction. Grandma had very traditional values. She would probably balk at the idea of them even talking about marriage after just knowing each other for less than a year and still not having their first date.

No doubt, her father may have a few words because Simon didn't come to him first. Those were all things Karleigh figured they would have to get over. Her life was hers to lead and do as she wanted.

Simon arrived at her house right on time and met her at the door with a single red rose. Karleigh was seeing him in a whole new light. She was allowing herself to really drink in the man that stood before her. He was gorgeous, and he wanted to marry her. That made her giggly inside.

"We may be doing this backward, but I still intend to wine and dine you. Flowers, chocolates, and everything. Even after we are married." Simon kissed her cheek and led her to his vehicle. He was driving his super huge SUV, and Karleigh needed assistance getting into the truck.

They preferred the silence of the car on their way to church. Neither of them saying much, just smiling and blushing on both of their parts.

Praise and worship was just starting when they arrived. Instead of sitting with her sisters, they opted for the back row. They didn't want to cause a scene, and knowing her sisters, one of them would do just that.

Another Sunday service where the pastor was speaking directly to the new couple. The sermon was about following your heart. Simon and Karleigh could both relate to following your passion, following your dream, and following your heart.

After service, Karleigh and Simon waited for her family to meet them in the rear of the church. Kyna was the first to approach and the first to see the ring.

"OH MY GOD! Is that what I think it is?" Her voice increasing an octave, she screeched, "Is that what I think it is?" Kyna started dancing around and grabbed Karleigh's hand.

Poe and Karmyn raced over at the commotion Kyna was making. When they saw the ring, they joined in with Kyna's hysterics.

Her sisters calmed down when their parents and grandmother joined the group. The sisters got quiet, awaiting the reaction of their father. He smiled and patted Simon on the back.

"Good job, young man. Are you sure you want to join this family?"

"Absolutely, sir."

"Thank you," Kevin said, relieved. "I won't be the only man in the family anymore."

"Dad, you're not upset he didn't ask you first?" Karmyn asked her father.

"What makes you think he didn't?" Kevin winked at Simon and left the women to continue to gawk over Karleigh's ring.

Instead of going to Karleigh's parent's house for dinner, Simon treated everyone to dinner at the Greenwich Steak House, where grandma Hammond grilled Simon about his life and his family. Simon didn't mind answering any of her questions. He felt a sense of peace, even when talking about his sister.

Telling everyone why he left a lucrative career in tech to open a barbershop didn't seem as bizarre as people made him feel in the past. He was proud of his decisions then and now. Karleigh was everything he needed, and he hoped he was the same for her.

*****

Two months after the engagement, Simon was sitting in Serenity, waiting for Karleigh to finish with her client. A young, attractive woman walked in and practically begged Karleigh to fit her into her schedule. Simon was planning to take Karleigh to see a musical and then to dinner. He patiently waited, hoping they wouldn't take much longer.

"Karleigh, you are absolutely magic. Thank you so much," the lady gushed while looking in the mirror at her hair.

"You're welcome. But, like I told you earlier, you didn't need much done."

"Maybe not. I have something to give you and Mr. Sharpe." The lady pulled two envelopes from her purse and handed them over. Simon and Karleigh were confused and didn't know what to make of things.

"Go ahead and open them. My name is Felicia McNary. I am an attorney for The Dorsey Brothers." She reached into her purse and pulled out two, crisp one-hundred-dollar bills. She handed them to Karleigh. "I meant what I said, you worked magic on my hair. This is for you. I'll call you next week to make an appointment. Goodnight." Felicia left them in shock.

Together, they ripped into their envelopes and read the letter from inside. The letters were identical. Grandma Hammond and Ms. Norma had set them up from the very beginning. With help from The Dorsey brothers, they were able to get the two of them to meet. But, they hadn't anticipated the drama that would unfold.

Grandma Hammond thought it was time her granddaughters found love before they were too old to have children. She knew it would be a challenge, so she enlisted the help of her good friend Ms. Norma. They focused their attention on Karleigh since she was the oldest.

When Mr. Dorsey overheard their plans one day, he mentioned it to his brother, who, in turn, had the perfect man in mind. The four of them plotted to push the two unsuspecting adults together. The Dorsey's intentionally made sure the business space Karleigh needed for her salon was a deal she couldn't refuse. Grandma Hammond knew the first time she met Simon that he was precisely the man Karleigh needed in her life.

Their letters also vehemently denied the actions of Alicia Whitsett and Ms. Carter, but they were happy that it pushed them together. The couple also found out the building had been sold to a trust set-up for them. The trust fund had stipulations that required the two of them to marry within three years. Karleigh believed that was her grandmother's doing.

Their envelopes also included the deed to their building and an engagement gift of $50,000. Karleigh held her envelope tightly to her chest and silently prayed. "Thank you, God, for always looking out for me and having your own plan."

Simon was still puzzled. How did any of them know their paths would meet, unless… "How did you find out about this building being available?" Simon asked Karleigh.

"My grandmother told me about it. When I inquired, the deal was too good to be true."

Karleigh and Simon remained silently for a few minutes, coming to the conclusion that the building was a part of the plan. Instead of getting angry, the two of them smiled and thanked God that the scheme of a few friends worked in their favor. They were the happiest they had ever been.

ABOUT THE AUTHOR

Lisa Washington is a Detroit native currently residing in Georgia with her family. Education is vital to her success, having earned degrees from Wayne State University, an MBA from Averett University, and an MFA from Butler University.

Lisa Washington is a serial entrepreneur and co-founder of The Washington Way LLC, with her husband, Markel Washington. Their company includes Washington Way Financial, Washington Way Publishing, Washington Way Travel, and Ms. Lisa Weddings.

I hope you enjoyed reading about Karleigh and Simon. I can't wait for you to read more about Poe, Kyna and Karmyn. Stay connected with us for new releases, exclusive offers, free online reads and so much more.

Subscribe to my newsletter
www.authorlisawashington.com

Don't forget to follow and like us on
Facebook - @authorlisawashington
IG - @authorlisawashington
Pinterest - authorlisawashington

My Sister's Keeper Series

Kaleigh – A Story of Patience

Kyna – A Story of Love

Karmyn – A Story of Hope